For my father, Edward; and my brother, Michael.
There is no heaven for me without the three of us together…as a family.

This book is a work of fiction. The characters, incidents and dialogue are products of the author's imagination and are not intended to bear any resemblance to actual events, or to historical persons (living, dead or otherwise) except where they are. Any such resemblances are coincidental, and purely for the purposes of providing historical context for completely fictional events.

Ascendent Publishing

1640 Worcester Avenue, D613, Framingham MA 01702

www.ascendentpublishing.com

ISBN 9781963970029

ἀρσε

V L K Ó Ç

w.p. quigley

your life is your life
don't let it be clubbed into dank submission.
be on the watch.
there are ways out.
there is a light somewhere.
it may not be much light but
it beats the darkness.
be on the watch.
the gods will offer you chances.
know them.
take them.

you can't beat death but
you can beat death in life, sometimes.
and the more often you learn to do it,
the more light there will be.
your life is your life.
know it while you have it.
you are marvelous
the gods wait to delight
in you.

"The Laughing Heart" – *Charles Bukowski*

Τηε Σαμε Ριϖερ Τωιχε
(the same river twice)

Dawn began to break as it always did...

...at the instant when Andreas, laying prone upon the soft, damp silt at the river's edge and staring straight into the boundless depths of infinite night, could discern that the sky above had shifted one shade lighter than the black sapphire of evening - the first whisper from a morning spectre.

If this had been a singular experience, just the mere promise of this procession of majesty in the heavens would have taken the breath from even the most cynical of observers. Andreas remained motionless, however, as this had been routine for him for longer than he could remember.

And it was always the same each morning, with naught so much as a slight deviation, in either the spectrum of colors that presented themselves upon the upper skin of the world or in their order or even in their duration upon that atmospheric stage.

The entirety of the beauty contained in the universe upon a single canvas, and Andreas had looked upon it far too many times and for far, far too long. He felt...nothing. Had felt nothing for how many mornings? How many days? How many nights? They were beyond counting in their combined numbers.

7

And this, then, was the greatest sadness and despair of all, which is to say that neither of those feelings in of themselves were present in his heart but rather - the absence of all stirring, all sensation, and all stimulus when he looked upon the divine.

Not far from where Andreas lay as a corpse would at its funeral, a message etched in rough granite promised all who continued on they would find it; the promise had been kept.

For here, indeed, was woe.

Chris had been banging on his older brother's apartment door for a solid ten minutes before finally running dry of every drop of patience he possessed. Which, not coincidentally, was a much smaller amount when it came to anything to do with his only sibling, his older brother Dante. It was then he let loose with a string of profanity loud enough to be heard by people passing on the street just outside of the building.

"FUCKING DANTE! WHAT THE FUCK?! IT'S TEN PAST ELEVEN! LET'S-"

Chris heard the rattling, dragging sound of a lock chain being dragged through and then out of its metal guide, followed by the quick click of a deadbolt release. The front door then swung open, revealing Dante defiantly standing there - clad only in a pair of Fruit of the Loom tighty-whities. He had his trademark shit-eating grin on full blast as well. It was like Dante was the stupidest X-Man of all, and his mutant superpower was a heightened shamelessness to the point of invulnerability.

"Kid, you were being serious last night when you said you wanted to start cleaning up Dad's condo today?"

"No, Dante, I was totally joking. What I really wanted more than anything was an excuse to drive

9

down to this demilitarized zone of a neighborhood you live in to spend some more real quality time with you. Can I come in, please, or am I gonna stand out in the fucking hallway all day?"

At that moment, a garbled yet shrill woman's voice rang out from somewhere in the apartment behind Dante.

"Sweetie? Are you coming back to bed?"

Dante's Cheshire Cat countenance disappeared.

"Uh, yeah Chris. Maybe now isn't the best-"

Chris pushed past the human dildo before him and marched into the room beyond, a kitchen that hadn't been cleaned in what had to have been no less than a month - judging by the mountain of moldy, food-covered dishes in the sink, and the filthy countertops. The entire apartment reeked of next-morning hard alcohol fumes and awful, sweaty four a.m. fucking. He knew where Dante's bedroom was from previous descents into the inferno that his brother called home and made his way directly to it. Sitting up in his bed with her floppy and fully exposed overweight girl's tits hanging on the left and right sides of her torso was one of the function hall's waitstaff that had been working during the reception yesterday.

She didn't even bother to cover herself up, instead deigning to flash a sheepish grin and acknowledge Chris's presence with a 'hi, there' wave of her hand.

Chris recalled her name, Violet, from the tiny, rectangular name tag that had been pinned to her work shirt the night before.

"Hey Violet? Dante has important shit to do right now, so if you could, please get dressed and uh, you know, fuck right off, please."

Chris closed the bedroom door. He turned to his left to see his brother flashing him double middle-fingers.

"I love you too, fuckface. Go say goodbye to yourplaymate and get your shit together. I want to get this done so I can move on with my life."

"Boy scout," Dante replied.

"Reject," Chris countered.

Andreas of Mycenae lifted his upper body up from the ground of the riverbank by pushing off the oversaturated earth underneath with both hands. In doing so, his fingers sunk into salt, slime, and earth deep enough to discern the temperature difference between the warmer mud at the surface and that which sat a few inches below the top.

His cue to do this was feeling the waters of the river against his skin as the tide neared full high. He'd noticed that his heels had become fully submerged, while a gentle lapping began to tickle to the lowest parts of his calf muscles. Andreas mused that it must have been the marked discrepancy in the two sensations - each originating from a single source - that stirred him at last to move some part of his body.

By the time Andreas mustered enough willpower to sit upright, the heavens above had long since reverted back into its nighttime hue of blue obsidian. It had been as if both morning and afternoon paraded past the man yet still hidden, undetected. Each moved as thieves that made no effort to conceal themselves, knowing their mark paid no attention to their machinations. Time wasn't stolen from him, for a thing that held neither meaning nor value could never be pilfered in any semblance of the definition.

Andreas gazed across the river. At first, he could discern nothing but vague silhouettes of its topography, the outlines of which were just pencil sketches set upon a background that was somehow both charcoal and a dim shade of cobalt. In both of their presences seen in equal quantities, a third color arose - one that could only be accurately described as that point on the spectrum where pure sorrow could be discerned. It was a sadness that obscured everything save for the suggestions of form.

And then, like fireflies performing an alien choreography, the illuminated but featureless shapes of fourteen, maybe fifteen humans appeared in formation. Their arrival upon that distant shoreline completed within just a single tick of the second hand of a clock.

Set against this backdrop of endless, infinite veil that likely was the dominant hue of a vacant soul, the figures each cycled through their own unique sequence of the secondary colors. These were intricate codings of purple, orange, and green so vivid and so brilliant, Andreas allowed himself a single moment of pure wonder. This, in spite of the interminable apathy he'd only just taken shaken off by rising from the ground.

Andreas said aloud:

"Mine would possess such magnificent violets that the others would forget themselves and behold my own majesty..."

Something about his pronouncement seemed off.

"...for violet was always my favorite of all the-"

He stopped. This last...was wrong. It wasn't true. Hadn't been true. Andreas turned his countenance away from the distant display downwards toward the ground just before him.

"I..."

He struggled to remember himself, who he was, who he had been. Had he entirely forgotten?

No.

"I am Andreas of Mycenae."

(murderer!!!!) (what?)

"I am Andreas of Mycenae!"

(a man who had raped his own sister)

14

He stood up, shouting at the luminous figures.

"I AM ANDREAS OF MYCENAE!"

None seemed to hear, much less acknowledge his plea.

(He hated the color violet, he hated the glowing ghosts, he hated all people and all things as he was executed in the field for his litany of transgressions)

Then why did he...

But then – just then.

In his mind.

He could see a passageway open.

No, that was not right. It was a door. A bulkhead? Total darkness, then blinding sunlight.

Greedy hands, taking. Taking arsenics and coppers *(bronze)*, coppers and arsenics *(bronze)* in turn. They shone like twin lighthouses; beacons he could use to find his way back.

So it was true. Andreas smiled. The figures finished their procession and vanished as quickly as

15

they appeared. They could go as the gods had ordained for them.

But he..he could defy the gods.

He could defy even...

Him. He who was not a god.

Twin lighthouses of the purest bronze called to him. He would answer, gladly.

Andreas found he could visualize the way back to the gates, the ruinous portal of suffering it was. Basalt, rusted iron, crumbling steel, worthless words etched into worthless materials.

Upon seeing those cursed gates in his mind once again, he had an identical reaction to it as the first time he beheld it with his eyes – this was the overwhelming urge to punish the artisans and craftsmen who'd constructed them as they in turn had punished him. He would murder them, each and all, with the stone and steel with which they'd fashioned the structure untold millennia prior to his arrival.

He grimly thought to himself:

16

I might still have the chance to do so. What better way to mark my return?

Andreas stood up on the riverbank and held his arms aloft. He instinctively knew all he needed to do: stretch out, hands to the sky and call out to those twin beacons with whatever remained of his own willpower.

Would it be enough?

Andreas reared back and dug within himself to make it enough.

That world in which he'd been satisfied enough simply to lay down in the filth, sludge, and slime and pass all of eternity began to fade. His surroundings turned from opaque to ghostly. Then at last, pockets of true transparency began to appear. He deigned to peer directly into one of these spaces, all shaped like human-sized gyres.

Something coming straight at him, faster than the most powerful, quickest, and strongest of predators he'd ever laid eyes upon.

It was made of metal, polished, and painted and expertly made; of glass shaped into a kind of stylized mirror or window. Andreas then saw a thing his mind rejected as hallucination the instant he saw it.

17

A human being - a woman, even - was piloting the thing.

The darkness across the river from those bound for the Elysian Fields vanished, and in its absence, it left an imprint, white, in the shape of a man not unlike the trace of a body at a crime scene.

And those illuminated figures disappeared as well, save for one. This lone soul's light flickered from those dynamic shades it shone with previously, to then glow deep and dark with the unmistakable color of crimson.

It took Dante a full hour to pull himself together enough to be able to help his brother. The day before, he'd reassured Chris multiple times he would - both before and after the funeral.

He really did want to help Chris and bang out the chore of retrieving valuables, personal effects, and any other items of import from their father's place. But just because Dante agreed to the plan and didn't immediately tell Chris 'no fucking way' the first time he'd asked didn't mean that there'd be even so much as a trace of urgency on his part when the time actually came.

From the sorry state of affairs that Chris had found Dante mired in, it was obvious that the elder Poulos had drank and fucked his way into selective amnesia regarding their going to their father's condo that day.

Violet, for her part, was up and on her way in less than ten minutes, likely out of sheer embarrassment. On her way out the door, she moved towards Dante for a kiss goodbye.

"Hey honey once you're done gimme a call? I got the night off so I can just back over later."

"Yeah, will do," Dante replied.

"You have my number, right?" she asked.

"Yeah, you put it in my phone last night when we got back here, don't you remember?"

"Oh, yeah. Okay, bye, Dante." Violet glanced at Chris and immediately turned her head downwards once he made eye contact with her, embarrassed over the circumstances of their second meeting the day after their fathers' funeral.

Violet shut the door behind her, and the instant she did Dante set about deleting her number. Chris knew this and called his brother out immediately.

"You're fucking erasing it now, aren't you?"

"Yuuuuuuup."

Chris shook his head. "Don't forget to block it before you erase it, asshole."

"Blocked it last night."

"Outstanding. If there's nothing's else, then can we go Dante? We're already way behind."

"After you, boss," Dante replied, infusing a generous portion of sarcasm into the word 'boss' at the end.

The two of them walked to Chris' car, parked a minute's walk down the street from Dante's apartment and were off. Chris quickly turned on the radio and turned the volume up loud enough to discourage further conversation. It was unlikely, in his estimation, they'd be able to just talk without it lapsing into bickering.

But it was a matter of just three minutes into the ride to their destination before Dante unknowingly unpinned a grenade and dropped it onto the floor of Chris' car. He lowered the volume of the music a notch or two and merely asked a simple question.

"So how long of a ride we looking at bro?"

Which Chris quickly made the correct inference that Dante had no idea where their father lived, despite their father having lved in the same place for years.

Chris had always been more goal-oriented, ambitious, and responsible than Dante. Chris' insistence upon driving to their dad's place the morning after putting the man into the ground was evidence of this. And this was a quality he'd inherited from his father, the two of them sharing that type-A personality configuration that made their relationship far more facile in terms of their closeness as Chris grew older.

Not so with Dante, as his eventual apocalypse-level falling out with his father had been more a matter of a 'when', rather than an 'if'. This had occurred years before, yet Chris really only had an idea as to the extent and the damage that had been done as a result of it, with no real sense of the details thereof. T
he fact that Dante had no idea what town his father lived in - Scituate, Massachusetts, just over an hour drive from Fall River where Dante's apartment was - for the past two years spoke volumes as to the extent of the wreckage. Chris wanted to lash out, start yelling at his brother for not even knowing where Dad moved to or had lived since mom passed away, but thought the better of it.

"So...no idea where Dad lived, hunh?"

"South Shore someplace, Chris. No idea *what town*, kid. Not fuckin' important, because-"

"You guys weren't talking. I know. Well aware."

Dante sighed. He knew it was hard on the kid, being the go-between for two grown-ass adults but it wasn't like it was any one person's fault, the situation being what it was and how it ultimately ended.

"Anyway..."

Dante rolled down the window before he continued.

"Whatever connection me and Dad had before didn't have a chance of surviving.

He blamed me for all the problems we had as a family. You know that shit, kid."

"You didn't help things, Dante."

"Was I supposed to? It didn't seem like it could be helped."

"Maybe at least try to...I don't know. How about not make them worse."

"For what?"

"For who."

"For whom, you mean. You might be the bright boy, the organized and ambitious one... but holy shit kid your usage sucks sometimes."

Chris and Dante had both inherited their father's black hair and olive-skinned complexions, and as such could easily be mistaken for twins were it not for their ages. The only real physical difference between them was that Dante was a few inches taller. But their similarities as people stopped there. Their clashing personailities only facilitated their abilities to get under the other's skin.

Dante saw that his last statement and pedantry regarding his brothers' command of the English language had done just that. Dante had managed to piss Chris off enough to make his complexion flush with frustration.

He'd always tried to tell/teach his younger brother not to be so tightly wound - the people who kept themselves like that always, *always* went to pieces the fastest. Once someone found an 'in' on them, it was over. Chris wouldn't unwind himself at his urging, so Dante always took his shot to drop in a jab. If he wasn't gonna listen, he'd teach him the hard way.

But not the hardest.

Their father had learned it the hardest way possible when he dropped dead of a massive coronary in his office at work. The assholes Stavros

Poulos was negotiating with were ultimately the last people to speak to him while he was alive.

And Dante wasn't having that with Christos. No fucking way.

"For *whom*, then Dante."

"Is it y-"

Just then, Chris's cell phone rang. The sound of it was less a digital, synthetic alert and more an old-school, analog tone. Like an actual...

"For whom the bell tolls," Dante whispered under the sound of it, which came from Chris's car speakers and not just the device itself.

"What the fuck?" said Chris aloud. He pushed the answer button.

"Hello? Mr. Dunsmuir?"

"Ah, Mr. Poulos. So sorry to disturb you, so soon after your father's passing. We've had a...well...a bit of a situation come up that requires your immediate attention."

"You're not disturbing me, Mr. Dunsmuir. What's the situation you're referring to?"

"Best you come straight in, Mr. Poulos?"

Dante butted in.

"How about you cut the bullshit Dunkirk and just tell us?"

"That must be the other Mr. Poulos. Have we sobered up yet, Dante? Otherwise I'd just as soon as resolve this-"

"We'll be there directly, Mr. Dunsmuir. It's on the way to our father's house, after all. Should be there in about... twenty minutes."

"Ah good, see you both then."

The line disconnected. . Whoever this asshole was at Morningside, the 'situation' was a lot more serious than he was letting on.

Silence followed for the next few minutes before Chris finally broke it.

"Still not helping things, Dante."

"Yes, I was. You just didn't let me finish."

Contrary to the combined eloquence and imagination of all the poets, writers, and philosophers who have felt inspired enough to opine about its legendary existence, the Styx did reach an endpoint – at the underworld's lowest level. This place had been fashioned from a deeper darkness, one that the shadows of things cast when set upon the sheer surface of non-existence.

One that only two beings in all of creation could look upon and not descend into immediate and permanent madness. These beings held their counsels in that place when the occasion called for such a thing to happen.

This meeting marked only the second time the river had been used by Charon and Hades.

The figure that appeared there first, silent as always, used his oar to bring his ferry alongside the shore until it came to rest. How it came to rest, and what it rest upon, Charon could not say.

Regardless, he had never been any sort to dwell upon such things.

Charon waited alone for what seemed an eternity, even to the being who'd existed throughout far too many of them already. There was neither sound nor light present upon the scene.

Eventually, the one who had once styled himself "Lord of the Underworld" in the characteristic pomposity and arrogance of youth appeared - dressed shoulder-to foot in obnoxious, ivory-colored robes. A dull crimson aura pervaded Hades so that from a distance, one could make out their silhouettes - the aforementioned man in crimson, the man standing upon the boat in the same crimson, albeit far less bright. The man in the boat would only be visible in the light of the man upon the shore.

Some time before and purely by chance, Charon heard a word come from the lips of a mortal that must have arisen in one of the languages that came long after the zenith of the ancient Greeks. Upon hearing it, he'd instantly thought of Hades and let out a single, almost inaudible chuckle.

"My Lord Charon, it is good to see you once again," Hades stated, bowing to one knee before him.

Cunt, thought Charon. He said nothing.

"Still the scintillating conversationalist my lord, even after all the millennia," Hades wittered on.

It's like he can't help himself, Thanatos. Charon often thought to himself as if either or both of his older brothers were present therein.

Hades sighed.

"No need to dilly-dally with pleasantries, then."

Silence. Hades continued.

"For the first time in centuries, one has escaped our grasp."

Charon broke his silence at this last.

"My grasp. You are as much a prisoner here as they are, despite your standing."

"A mere formality, my lord."

Silence, again.

Hades grew angry with Charon's stubborn refusal to regard him as an equal even now - as could be seen by his aura, which shone brighter and a deeper shade of red.

"Well then, jailer, are you aware of *who* has escaped your grasp?"

"No, Hades, for that soul never came upon my vessel. He was sent to the afterlife without his fare, and so he remained upon the shores of Acheron. The soul had been there so long that - "

A single, laser-thin beam of the color of blood rocketed from the temple under the hood of the man in the boat. As quickly as it appeared, as quickly it vanished and once again, silence. He'd shown Charon who had just been loosed upon the world.

More appropriately:

What had been loosed.

Hades had started preparing himself for what was inevitable the moment he'd learned of the abomination's escape:

One of Charon's legendary, universe-shattering screams.

The particular one that Hades expected (for Charon's screams bore a certain variety to them) could not be mistaken or confused with any of the other kinds that had been heard throughout the underworld over the millennia. It was for this reason that Hades summoned the ferryman to this place, instead of any other. Down here, only Hades would hear the sound of Charon's rage.

Such a wail, such a sound, was unlike any scream in all of creation. The mere echo of this particular kind of howl could drive even a god insane. Hades had heard it, full throat, more times than even he could remember. He considered this, and thought to bring Charon here before delivering the news.

Despite his planning and forethought, the fabric of every plane - except that of the living - shook at its thunder.

Once it had ceased, Hades took a moment to regain himself. Charon was not a god. Was never a god. He'd always been something more – and at this moment, Hades had been reminded of that.

"What then, my lord Charon? Shall thee retrieve him?" Hades regaled in using overblown words of address, if only to annoy Charon.

Charon said nothing. His answer was implied by the lack of one.

"Then you must remember that since he has returned to the plane of mortals, he will have...changed. He will speak their language, and he will know their customs and manner of being. As will you, Lord Charon. You will not...appear as you have in previous sojourns."

31

Charon had already begun pushing off from the shore.

"You know how he has managed to escape, my lord! That silly loophole you adhere to, even after all the centuries and all the millennia. The coins surrendered to you for your fare."

Charon made haste and was already several yards away from the man on the shore.

"The man's coins that have been stolen from his place of rest. His name is..."

"Stavros Poulos," Charon whispered under his breath. "I know now, you pompous jackass."

Hades began to laugh at Charon, knowing that he'd exercised his one sliver of power over this being, shouted after him with what he should have told the ferryman before he'd departed.

"Lord Charon! If he remembers himself – when he remembers ARSENIKOS...he will be more than just a man! And you will only be..."

"Mortal, Hades!" Charon said.

I'm aware of that aspect, too. Cunt.

32

The car swerved out of the way of Andreas just in time to avoid hitting him dead on, but in doing so spun into several barrels of garbage that had been put out on the nearby sidewalk before grinding to a halt.

Andreas had not so much as a few seconds time to take in his new surroundings before the driver of the car got out and ran towards him, still standing out in the street.

Buildings, made of concrete, impossibly tall. The roads...smooth, painted. The smell was atrocious – like oil and trash had somehow merged with waste and shame. A glimpse at sign named the city in which he stood. It had been written in a language he shouldn't have understood, and yet he could hear the words spoken inside his head as he looked upon them.

Fall River.

And then the girl was upon him.

He looked upon her, a pathetic, overweight thing with dirty blond hair and soiled clothing. She'd been the whore of one of the men he sought just the evening before. Foul creature.

33

Wait.

Something occurred to Andreas in that second:

Why such immediate disdain for this person who'd just managed to avoid killing him? Shouldn't he be grateful? Thankful for her-

"Jesus fucking Christ, asshole, get out of the fucking street you'll get yourself killed!" she exclaimed, practically screaming in his face.

He wanted nothing more to snap her neck then and there.

Instead, Andreas flipped into a role, a staged persona, with the best acting he could muster. After all, he had once been an actor, had he not? The finest in all of Mycenae. This character he played had been one often used in heyday - 'confused old foreigner'.

"Oh, I'm so sorry miss! I seem to have – I'm sorry! I'm quite lost. I've lost my...I've lost my cat..."

Andreas was at as loss for the cat's name. He glanced over Violet's shoulder. He spotted a sign, an advertisement for ***Big Al's Auto Repair & Transmission*** behind her. He quickly improvised.

34

"My cat Alphonse...and I'm just...I'm just..." and at this, Andreas broke down into an unfettered burst of tears and emotion. The performance of a lifetime.

The woman ceased her bellowing and reconsidered the situation.

"Oh, sir. Oh, I'm so so, so sorry!"

She looked up and down the street in either direction, likely scanning to see if there had been any witnesses to what had just occurred. Fortunately, there were none.

"Let's get you off the street before we both get run over!" The girl took Andreas by the elbow and led him back over to where her car had veered off the street.

"Is this...is this city where you live, Miss..."

She had no intention of giving this man her last name.

"Oh, you can call me Violet, sir."

Violet. Of course. His means of escape had been telegraphing itself into his mind before he became fully aware of it.

He HATED violet.

"Violet, oh thank you so much. Were it not for your quick action I might be dead on the street... and...and Alphonse..."

"Oh, I'm sure you're upset sir, especially losing your companion?"

"Yes...he's my only friend these days. Violet, I hate to bother you, but if you could? Please, I could just use a ride back to my home. It's just a few...oh dear. I'm so confused."

Andreas scanned his mind for the word these people used.

"...blocks back the way you came."

The girl, in her limited capacity for thought, must have rationalized that by giving him a ride back to his *(apartment)* home, she could avoid potential run-ins with the *(constabulary)* police.

"Um..." Violet seemed unsure.

"I mean, we should get out of here, you know, before the police show up. I don't think either of us want to deal with all their questions. Do you?"

The mere mention of their impending arrival pushed her in the direction he needed her to go.

"Oh, yeah of course. I mean, how awful would I be not giving an old man a ride back to his place? You can call animal enforcement and let them know there. Here..."

Violet beckoned to the passenger side of her chariot – (*car*) or (*automobile*) - and motioned for him to get into her car.

"Oh thank you, miss, thank you so much!"

Once inside, Andreas flipped down the (*visor*) visor. There was a mirror on the side that was not exposed. He had to take a look at himself. He'd even forgotten his own face, what he looked like.

There, he saw himself, only far, far older than he had been at the time of his death. Long, snow white hair. Olive, wrinkled skin. And eyes with no color, almost entirely black.

ARSENIKOS.

What was that word? It appeared in his mind upon seeing his face again for the first time in...how long? How long had he been marooned, forced to wile away eternity by that infernal river?

How had he died again?

He could not recall. Regardless, the man he saw was a wizened man, of no less than sixty years of age. He could recall that he had been much, much younger at the time of his death. How had it -

Violet got into the driver's side and quickly maneuvered her car onto the street and forward.

How fast this vehicle could travel!

Andreas studied her actions and movements as she turned the vehicle around and in the opposite direction from which she came. And, by doing so, quickly ascertained how to drive and operate this 'car'.

"Where do you live, mister?"

"Andreas, my dear. You can call me Andreas."

It's just up here, on the right. You can pull into the..." (*parking lot*) "parking lot behind my building." He motioned towards his apartment.

"Okay, sure thing Andreas," she glanced over at him, smiling a nervous grin. He smiled back. He'd since shut his scared old man waterworks off as if they came from a (*faucet*) faucet.

"Thank you, Violet. Such a pretty name! And - my favorite color too."

"Really, Andreas?"

"Really, my dear."

Violet did as she was bidden, pulling into an empty lot behind the building Andreas had gestured towards.

Andreas scanned the surroundings in a less than second and saw there was not a soul in sight. It was as if one of the other gods were helping his escape from his unceasing existence on the shores of the afterlife instead of within it. This was meant to be then!

"Mister I really ho - "

Andreas gave Violet not another instant to continue her idiotic blathering. Striking with the speed of a serpent and the strength of a bull, Andreas stuck out his left arm and took Violet by the hair on the left side of head. He began smashing her skull over and over again into the glass and the window on the other side of it. The force of the first blow alone fractured her skull, knocking her unconscious.

This was not enough for Andreas; for something about this act of wanton murder reminded him of...himself. Over and over again, he yanked Violet's head back from the window and then back into it, until a circular spider's web of fractured glass and sprayed blood, flesh, and bone formed. It was a lesson for her to learn, and she would learn it.

ARSENIKOS.

Andreas found that he had to will himself to cease turning the girl's face and skull into gory mockery of what they once were.

He leaned over, opened the door, and pushed Violet's corpse out of the car. Andreas closed the door
after her lifeless body fell onto the pavement with a thump. He then pushed his way into the drivers' seat.

He rolled down the window upon which Violet's life had ceased. He then turned the vehicle around in the parking lot, and hastily left the area.

Someone would discover her body - but how long would that take? Minutes? Hours? Andreas felt he had very little time. He could see the coins in his mind - they were at a place called Morningside Funeral Home. He would make haste there.

Chris pulled his Lexus into the parking lot at Morningside Funeral Home. When it was empty, and not filled with the vehicles belonging to mourners, well-wishers, and the like, it appeared enormous, vast – much larger than such a thing needed to be for a funeral home. Despite this, Chris drove towards one of the far corners of the lot and brought the car to a halt.

Pausing a moment, Chris anticipated what Dante was about to say.

"This fucking place creeps me the fuck out, Dante. That's why I parked all the way out here."

Dante laughed.

"I wasn't gonna say shit bro. Any other time? Yeah, what the fuck. We're like a quarter of a mile away from the front doors. But this place?" Dante looked over his shoulder back at Morningside.

"If I'm gonna criticize anything it's that you didn't park far enough away from the place. Fucking look at it. It's like a cheesy seventies' horror movie brought to life."

Chris looked over his shoulder at the structure as well.

"Let's get this over with," Chris added. Dante nodded in agreement.

Chris and Dante got out of the car and made their way to the funeral home where they'd spent most of the previous forty-eight hours mourning their father.

Charon arrived on Earth with no fanfare, no burst of lightning, sound, or fury. One second, empty air. The next a figure, dressed in a black tee-shirt and regular, unremarkable blue jeans. Upon his forearms were matching tattoos, his symbol, inked in a medium shade of purple - magenta perhaps.

This pleased him.

In each hand he held one of his preferred weapons - the *sagaris*. They were a combined battle axe and war hammer the Greeks first encountered in their battles with the Persians. By the time they had been adopted into their own arsenals, the blunt end had been adopted into a sharpened point meant for piercing.

He regarded them fondly, thankfully. For an instant he held the fear that as he stepped across Pyriphlegethon and into the realm of mortals - that these tools would be supplanted by some silly, modern implements of death. However, his tools held special properties here, and could not be replicated by something as crude and primitive as a firearm.

At last, he surveyed his surroundings. An area where many mortals lived within dwellings called...

43

condominiums. Charon mused that Arsenikos' head would likely be reeling from the constant barrage of new knowledge – and vocubulary – that he did not experience. The mortal's mind functioned like a funnel in this circumstance; those born of higher planes were like high-powered transmitters and receivers.

An insipid, convulted word for something as simple as a home. Still, it is where Stavros Poulos had made his home, and it would be here that Charon would lie in wait for the fugitive.

One last measure of his present to be taken then. He glanced around and found a puddle of muddy water in which he could see what countenance his face had taken. He bore no cloak - no hood either with which to hide his true face. What then, had replaced it?

Lord Charon walked over to the ersatz mirror and looked down upon his reflection. Instead of his face and head shrouded and obscured by hood and shadow, he saw that both were covered entirely by a matted, aubergine, knitted skullcap that had been woven large enough to cover one's face as well. It had been fashioned such that eyeholes had been cut into the garment, but covering those spots where his eyes should have appeared were something called *(welder's goggles)* welder's goggles. They were

44

outlandishly large, perfectly circular lenses that were darkened such that his eyes, his *true* eyes could not be seen behind them.

This was...adequate. Perhaps he could even grow to prefer them over his torn, weathered black cloak and hood.

There was something else too - his physical body. No longer was he an ancient, wizened, impossibly old man. In the underworld, his flesh hung on his bones like the cloak and hood he wore hung upon his shoulders. His body, his frame was...young. It was folly to attempt to deduce or infer this form's exact age, but Lord Charon could feel strength - actual strength - course through his arms and legs. He could even run, a thing which the last time he had done so eluded even his infinite memory. He mustn't let this form delude him from its fragility.

But then Charon noticed the horns atop his brow. He reached up, grazed them both with the back of his left hand. He felt them as if they were a part of him, and not some adornment. Curious. Would this world see him as some sort of beast? A demon, a spirit, as...evil?

Charon let air puff through his nostrils and through his mask. Mortals. They had always seen him as malevolent. And yet he had always taken great care of them.

In all the millennia upon millennia, malice, harm, and belligerence were things he had never felt towards another living creature. Since he'd lost Thanatos and Hypnos on the day of their adulthood there was only one emotion Lord Charon ever experienced, for he had been, was, and would forever be...

alone.

Upon pushing open the gothically themed and needlessly oversized double doors again for a third consecutive day, Chris and Dante strode through the main receiving room at first but then stopped short, as if ordered by silent command. They'd practically lived in this monument to architectural overkill for the past forty-eight hours and yet the interior felt entirely alien to both of the Poulos brothers at that moment.

The causation for this feeling was quite simple, but Chris and Dante could not put their finer on the exact nature of it. As the two of them stood there, frozen in place, it represented the first time that the entirety of their emotions and thoughts weren't consumed or directed towards the process of grieving.

The space left behind was filled with a far closer to normal amount of awareness - of themselves and their surroundings.

The couches and chairs where the Poulos family took respite, reeling from the loss of one their patriarchal figures were instead furnishings upon which hundreds, maybe thousands of asses had sat. These funerary accouterments possessed the kind of bizarro-world odor that was produced by having been cleaned nearly as many times they'd been sat and by as many different chemicals as families that had retained Morningside's services.

But it wasn't the furnishings that reeked of the most fetid aromas of humanity, covered over with enough perfume-scented soaps, shampoos, and polishes to cover each of them up.

In the air, the unmistakable aroma of formaldehyde had mingled inexorably with the oxygen and nitrogen that desperately wanted out of the funeral home as well. It was the smell of aromatic, hydrocarbon-infused death.

"I feel like we just checked into a hotel room where a triple homicide went down last night and the cleaners literally just left," said Chris.

"This place is like a museum dedicated to shitty carpeting, sweaty slacks, and polyester farts," opined Dante.

The two exchanged a look after their assessments of Morningside, no longer in a completely overwhelmed state-of-mind, and both began laughing hysterically.

Dante put his hand on Chris's shoulder. "Kid, this fucknut better get his ass -"

From behind them, Dunsmuir cleared his throat. The brothers spun around, unsure of how much the man had heard.

"Gentlemen, right this way. I'm just as eager to get this business over with as you apparently are." Dunsmuir spun around as if an enlisted man performing an about face, and with his six-foot-plus height and ghostly white hair pulled backwards, the man was more like the butler at Wayne Manor if Batman and Alfred both were undead. He sure as hell didn't convey 'proprietor of a middle-class suburban funeral parlor' with his presence.

Dunsmuir led Chris and Dante into his office and gestured towards the bare wooden chairs positioned in front of his desk. They sat down in them, experiencing immediate discomfort while Dunsmuir took a seat in a polished leather high-back.

Dunsmuir surveyed them both, sighed, and then pulled open the center drawer of his desk. He produced a letter-sized manila envelope, undid the metal clasp, and emptied it onto the blotter.

Out of that giant envelope dropped two shiny, silver-colored coins.

Chris regarded them silently but remained emotionless. But Dante rocketed out of his chair in

49

such a sudden, violent flurry of movement that he knocked his chair backwards onto the ground.

"ARE YOU FUCKING KIDDING ME, DUNSMUIR?!?"

Both Dunsmuir and Chris were frightened into full fight-or-flight responses, not so much as from Dante's outburst or his threatening stance, but that the entire display came from Dante. For Dunsmuir's part, he'd expected something like this once they'd been informed of the violation of their father's resting place, just not from the older of the two. This one had spent every waking moment in a state of intoxication so elevated that he gave the impression he was but a single drink away from passing out. But here he was, ready to tear his fucking throat out.

After Chris' initial state of alarm had dropped enough, his first feeling was that of complete confusion.

"Jesus Dante, they're just a couple of coins, it's not like they're worth millions or anything."

Dante spun on his younger brother with a ferocity and anger he hadn't seen from him since they were teenagers fighting over the same girl in high school.

"Not about the money, zipperhead. Dad needs those with him if he's going to be able to rest."

"Oh, my God," replied Chris.

"Not exactly."

"You actually believe the same nonsense Dad did? Greek mythology? For real?"

"Ya. I've always said so, haven't I? A lot."

"Dante, I thought you were just drunk."

Dante only continued to glare at his brother, and a brief spell of quiet ensued.

Dunsmuir broke it before it could go on for any longer than just a few seconds.

"Gentlemen, the ceremony - and the graveyard - where your father was interned was Christian. I don't understand how this in any way affects Mr. Poulos' eternal -

Again, Dante turned upon the speaker of stupidity, this time Dunsmuir, and launched another ferocious verbal assault.

"Dooshmuir. They don't exactly have plots of land set aside for the dead followers of fucking Poseidon and Zeus now, do they?"

Chris felt as if he didn't try to restore sanity to the room now, it'd end up with Dunsmuir unconscious on the floor and Dante getting dragged away in cuffs.

Wouldn't be the first time he'd had a front row seat at that circus, either. Chris asked, in a subdued tone, what exactly had occurred.

Dunsmuir, visibly horrified at the prospect of having both orbital bones smashed into fine powder by Dante's sinewed fists, stuttered to answer the inquiry. Dunsmuir could only think of a neanderthal possessing such appendages.

Chris put his hand on his brother's forearm. "Dante, sit down. Mr. Dunsmuir, go on." Dante relaxed at last, turned around and picked his chair up off the floor.

"The vandal - thief - that is, is a groundskeeper who works almost exclusively at the cemetery itself, only occasionally performing light landscaping here around the home. I prefer to take care of the presentation of everything when it comes to Morningside," A pause. It was clear that Dunsmuir expected some kind of recognition for his superlative attention to detail, but he certainly wasn't going to get it from either of the Poulos brothers at the moment.

Dunsmuir continued:

"The running theory is that he'd caught sight of coins on your father's face during the rites at the grave site. Then, once everyone had left and he was alone to carry on the actual burying of the casket, he saw his opportunity and pilfered the bronze coins then."

Dante and Chris exchanged a look of bemused confusion. Dunsmuir was old, but he certainly didn't seem like he was even remotely close to senility or even early-stage dementia. Guy was sharp as a tack.

"Mr. Dunsmuir, the coins my father insisted be placed in his coffin are silver, not bronze," Dante picked one of them off the desk blotter and held it up.

"See? Silver."

Dunsmuir smiled and looked over to Chris to see if the calmer and more level-headed of the two knew the actual material of the coins' composition, but it was clear from his prideful, you-tell-em look he was flashing both his big brother and Dunsmuir he did not.

"Gentlemen, the coins appear silver in color, but assure you they are fashioned out of bronze. One of the earliest forms of the alloy ever to appear...well, in history."

The look of confusion re-appeared on the brothers' face, only this time it was genuine confusion.

Chris spoke up.

"What do you mean, Mr. Dunsmuir? We always thought that..."

"They were silver? No, Christos, that is most certainly not the case. Early forms of bronze were alloys of copper and arsenic, not tin. Raw copper ore is often naturally found contaminated with arsenic, but only maybe a percent or so of the total weight of the ore."

"Regardless, early metallurgists, alchemists, and most important, smiths – realized that the removal of the arsenic impurity resulted in the weaker, purer copper. So instead of taking it out, they experimented with how much arsenic should be left

54

in the alloy to maximize the overall strength of the final product."

"How much – " was all Dante got out before Dunsmuir cut him off.

"I don't know the exact percentage, Dante, I'm a funeral home director. But I do know that there's a high enough point where elemental arsenic leaches out. A bit lower than that is likely where the amount of arsenic was left."

Chris already wanted to wrap this left turn into the origins of fucking bronze up and get on their way and cut off the dissertation before it could stretch any further. He knew where it was going, and he knew how Dante would react. A moment ago he was ready to beat Dunsmuir to a pulp over the tradition being broken. The next would probably find him thinking about selling both coins for rent money or even worse, drugs.

"So what," Chris said, as he picked up one coin and pocketed it and handed the other to Dante, "my dad had these specially made then?" He finished his question by standing up as if to leave. Dante took the second coin, then merely looked at his younger brother as if to say, 'we in a rush all of a sudden?'

"No, Christos, that would be quite impossible, as no jeweler or craftsman would even attempt to even try to create arsenical bronze because of the risks involved."

Dante stood up, his anger having since been replaced by genuine curiosity and interest into what Dunsmuir was telling them.

"So what you're saying is that these coins are old as f-"

Chris grabbed Dante's arm and yanked as hard as he could in the direction of the exit from Dunsmuir's office.

"Let's go Dante. Now."

Dunsmuir stood up, stepping after them as Chris began forcing his brother out with him.

"I should say so, Dante. But does this mean that you both will not be proceeding with any legal matters against either myself or the home..."

Chris answered for the both of them.

"Nope, good work, Mr. Dunsmuir, thank you so much."

Andreas opened his eyes and looked in the direction of the glowing numbers located in the center of the panel that contained most of the vehicle's controls. The illuminated readout gave 2:15 as the time. This was comforting to him not just knowing the precise time, but also learning that even the citizens of this strange new nation kept the measure of their days and nights in the same manner his own people had, albeit more precisely and with the aid of their advanced technologies.

He had driven then, for thirty minutes guided by something called GPS that showed the path before. It was a remarkable thing, really, but he could also see how reliance upon it would build dependence, and so it must be that these...Americans would be lost without it at their disposal.

He had left the body of the girl Violet at two, which meant that he had spent the difference - a full fifteen minutes - with the car stopped and pulled off to the edge of the road.

The influx of information and knowledge of this world began at a trickle upon his 're-birth'. Single words at first, just to communicate with Violet. She'd considered herself respectable, of at least a status above that of the lowest. The girl was fooling herself - her purpose in life was to serve others, nothing more, nothing less. He'd done her a favor by snuffing out her life's flame before the lines, the wrinkles, and all the indignities she'd suffer as the years would systematically render her existence that much more desperate and pathetic as they went on.

But what started with words like 'automobile' and 'apartment', 'parking lot' and 'GPS', the meanings of which were easy enough to discern one or two at a time as they appeared in his mind, was quickly replaced by a full *download* of this culture, its technology, and its advances. The feeling was that of a mental dam being forced open, broken apart with massive **sagaris** like the Spartans had begun wielding after their battles with the Persians.

What tripped him up, made him incapable of keeping up with the massive influx of facts, images, words... everything... wasn't the sheer amount of information, however. It was this culture's surprising steps backwards into darkness and ignorance, even thousands of years after he...

-ARSENIKOS-

...the great Andreas of Mycenae had lived. What society rejects artistic and academic excellence in favor of-

58

Wait.

What was that word before his name?

Just then, there was rapping upon the metal roof of the car, not one made by a hand but one by treated, hardened wood. A baton.

Andreas looked to his left and saw a man, uniformed *(police officer)* leaning down into the open window to make eye contact with him. Another glance further left

and downwards revealed the location of the police officer's preferred weapon – his pistol.

Andreas then looked into the man's eyes for a moment, and in that tiny amount of time he realized he was in the presence of a man who chose his profession for the power it afforded him, not in some altruistic bent to protect the common good.

-YOUR KIND OF MAN, ARSENIKOS.-

Andreas shook his head, confused again by that voice that had made its second appearance in less than a minute.

"How we doin' today, sir?" the officer asked.

"Um, fine, officer. Just – just not feeling well at the moment. I had to pull over."

"You been drinking at all today, sir?" asked the officer. Not a trace of sympathy and asking a question he already knew the answer to; the officer would have been able to smell drink on his breath the instant he approached the drivers' side window.

Andreas knew that...

-THAT'S NOT YOUR NAME-
\
he'd need to make quick work of this man and be on his way or else he'd never find the brothers or the coins.

"Uh, no, officer, not drinking. But if you wouldn't mind, may I step out of my vehicle just to get some air?"

"Was just about to ask you to do that very thing, sir," the officer said as he stepped backward from the door to allow Andreas egress to the exterior of the car.

As soon as Andreas opened the door, he launched into his performance of 'old man in need of physical assistance', stumbling over the seat belt first, then extending his arms to convey the impression he was having trouble keeping his feet. All to draw the officer in closer to him for the coup-de-gras.

The officer placed his baton on the roof of the vehicle and stepped forward, attempting to gently take Andreas by his arms to steady the man. It was exactly what Andreas had hoped he would do.

Within the span of less than a couple of seconds, Andreas slipped his left arm down to officer's right hip. He flipped the leather catch on the holster with his thumb, clicked the pistol's *(safety)* to its off position. He pointed the barrel at the policeman and then put three shots directly into his ribcage, the man's insides exploding behind him with each shot.

There was silence afterward, as the officer's eyes jerked wide open, at first from sheer surprise at what had just happened. They then closed as both his heart and life stopped, his torso torn apart by the hollow-tipped bullets he insisted on loading his firearm with.

Andreas smiled as the hapless idiot fell to the ground. The ones that sought power simply for power's sake were always blind to the ones that hid theirs under a cloak of weakness; it was then that they always, without fail, revealed the reason why having power meant so much to them:

It was because they were intrinsically, fatally flawed human beings.

Andreas felt as surge of adrenaline re-invigorate his senses, centering him and allowing him to regain his focus.

He quickly grabbed the officer's baton from the car's roof, flipped the gun's safety back to the 'on' position, and tossed both into the passenger seat of the vehicle. Climbing back into the driver's seat, Andreas fastened his seat belt and drove off – there wasn't another moment to lose.

"Dude, what the fuck?" started Dante the second they pulled out of the funeral home parking lot.

"What?" replied Chris.

"You know exactly *what*. The fuck's up with the whole 'we have to leave now' push and shove routine in Dunsmuir's office?"

"I thought you were gonna beat the poor guy to death, Dante."

"BULLSHIT, bro. You'd have started dragging me out of the office the second I kicked over my fucking chair if that was true. Nope. Instead, the second he started with the story with how rare and valuable Dad's coins might be, you went off with the whole let's go right now like someone lit your short and curlies on fuckin' fire. Now what gives?"

They pulled up to a four-way intersection just off the road that led to Morningside. Chris flipped on his blinker to take a left to head towards their father's.

"You're so fucking embarrassing sometimes Dante," replied Chris.

"What?"

"You're so embarrassing, I could tell you were about to absolutely humiliate yourself in front of fucking Dunsmuir right in that office and *I* couldn't let you do it."

Chris looked over at Dante, who'd already been distracted by something else despite how passionately

he'd started this argument. He was looking, even gawking at the vehicle to their right at the intersection.

"That's the same kind of car that Violet drives..."

"*HEY ASSHOLE. FOCUS.*" yelled Chris, his voice raised to a volume loud enough to snap his brother out of gawking at another car at the intersection. The light then turned green, so Chris made the left faster than he usually would have done.

"I fucking heard you, Chris. I'm an embarrassment. It's funny – dad's dead but I can hear his same words coming out of your mouth. Tell me something new, dude. Like maybe an original thought you might have had at some point today."

"Dunsmuir launched into that whole routine about the coins not being silver and instead being these ultra-rare, super valuable artifacts to throw you off of ripping his fucking throat out, Dante. Guy knew you'd forget all about tradition, dad's requests

64

for his burial, and all that the second he started spouting all of that bullshit."

"You think he was making it up?" asked Dante.

"Unequivocally. And you were falling for it hook, line, and sinker, too."

"Why would he do that, then genius? *Do* enlighten my ignorant ass."

"If we press whatever charges against the scumbag who lifted them out of dad's coffin, it means that the coins have to be submitted and held as evidence, Dante. He sells you this whole routine about how arsenic – fucking *arsenic* of all things was used in making bronze and look at that. Suddenly Dante doesn't give a shit about ritual or ceremony or dad's wishes and all he cares about now is selling the fucking coins for money for whatever."

Dante was silent. He was silent because his little brother was absolutely correct. And it hurt.

Chris saw the internal pain on his brother's face appear the second he inflicted it. He wasn't trying to be malicious. Wasn't trying to hurt him. He didn't mean to make him feel badly about himself – but Chris *did* want better for his brother, and not just in superficial things like apartments, possessions, and all that.

Chris wanted to see his brother be a better person, the one he knew he was capable of being – and he knew being delicate or nice about it wasn't going to get that done.

Dante took his cell phone out and began surfing the web, putting his head down as he did so. This was what Dante always did when shame ambushed him as it so often did. It always overwhelmed him.

At the next stop sign, Chris glanced over at Dante's cell phone to see what his brother was looking at instead of him.

It was the Wikipedia entry for bronze. He wanted to see if Dunsmuir really was yanking his chain, apparently.

Or he's trying to save some face, asshole, thought Chris. *You did just ruin the fucking guy.* It was Chris's turn to wrestle with personal shame. He said nothing more about it as he got the car moving again.

Chris continued to dwell upon his and Dante's exchange with Dunsmuir in the silence that followed. While replaying what had transpired less than a half hour ago in his mind (again), it occurred to Chris that Dante's conniption may have just been an act – a performance to put the old man on his heels for the duration of their conversation. He had to check. After all...Greek mythology? Who even thought any of that nonsense could be anything but utter bullshit.

"Dante?"

"What," he replied in a half-declarative, half-interrogative tone of voice.

"Do...do you really believe in all that bronze coins, afterlife, River Styx stuff?"

"Doesn't matter what I believe, Chris."

"C'mon. For real."

Dante became irritated. He was trying to focus on what he was reading on his cell phone screen.

"Dad believed it," he answered in the hushed tone of a person responding to a question only half-heard.

"What?"

And the moment had come when Dante snapped. He turned to his left, positioned his body such that his face was mere inches from his brother's right ear, and shouted directly into it.

"I SAID DAD FUCKING BELIEVED IT, YOU ARROGANT, DEAF LITTLE SHIT."

Dante settled back into the passenger seat as quickly as he'd risen from it to berate Chris. He resumed reading the Wikipedia article he'd only gotten a quarter of the way through before unleashing his brief, oddly controlled emotional detonation.

Chris had wanted to believe that Dante still loved their father enough as to literally leap to his defense - should his honor be even slightly besmirched. He received the answer he'd hoped he get, just not in the way he expected.

Chris remained silent after enduring the verbal assault. He'd wanted to say more - felt like he should say more. But it didn't seem like it'd do any good to say anything else, at least for the moment.

Fifteen minutes later and the Poulos brothers had at last arrived. The street sign to their left read "Pluto Lane". Between Dante taking an exorbitant amount of time to get his shit together and the stop-off at Morningside, the sky had already begun to darken, a fact which disgusted Chris, but Dante, lost in his internet research, failed to notice. They pulled into the condo complex proper when at last Dante finished his cell phone internet research and finally put his phone back into his pocket.

"Chris," he began.

"What?"

"Dunsmuir wasn't making anything up. Arsenic really was used in the first bronzes ever produced. The English word fuckin' comes from ancient Greek – *arsenikos*."

"Meaning what? Poison?"

"Nope. It's means masculine, male, virility. Guess that tracks with the whole strengthening the alloy shit Dunsmuir talked about."

"So what, Dante, am I supposed to apologize now for thinking that you were gonna make yourself look stupid,

one second championing dad's wishes and then the next salivating over how much you could sell them for?"

"At least I said something about it, Chris. You didn't give the slightest shit about what that scumbag fucking did."

Chris pulled into the spot in front of their father's two-story abode.

"Let's just get this over with, Dante. I'm happy you're with me to do this, and I don't want to let this turn into a reason we stop talking to each other, too."

69

"Fine, Chris." Dante paused. "Hey, Chris?"

"What, man?"

"*Arsenikos*. That word."

"What about it?"

"Don't you get it? Arsenic. Male. Our people fucking invented toxic masculinity milennia ago."

"Ha. Well. It's only toxic in the purest form, then."

"What? Like Joe Rogan? Andrew Tate?"

"No. Not them. Something else."

Lord Charon had been patiently waiting and watching from his hiding spot for just over an hour. At last, a car appeared in the road that joined this tiny village to presumably a main road. Charon narrowed his eyes to focus them, and in doing so spotted Christos Poulos driving the vehicle. His brother, Dante, must have been the one riding in the passenger side. Christos – he was called Chris by most – brought the vehicle to a stop. The two of them got out, and judging by the looks on their faces they appeared to have been bickering for hours.

Brothers.

Charon watched how they walked together, yet apart. Like magnets of the same polarity being held in proximity.

Brothers.

He thought of his own. Thanatos first, then Hypnos, and found himself cycling through those emotions seemingly reserved for that unique relationship.

Brothers.

His heart throbbed with pulses of fresh longing for them. They were among the masters of their universe, but they had been boys once, too. How they had loved each other then!

Brothers.

As they matured past childhood, they each took on their own qualties of character , the ones that inevitably led to conflicts. Then came anger with each other, all over those same conflicts, over things that seemed to mean so much at the time. All of then proved to be nothing more than small, petty, meaningless squabbles. How they each thought, so certainly, they had grown to genuinely hate each other over their battles.

Brothers.

Then, the yawning chasm of loss opened once more, the void where the absence of loved ones is never filled. Even the gods weren't immune to this particular source of pain.

Charon thought:

One papers it over to fool oneself that it isn't there instead of acknowledging it. One carries on with existence, only to find years later, when the paper peels back, the void has only grown larger.

Charon spun faster than one of Poseidon's typhoons and swung his *sagaris* in twin cutting motions into a maple tree that stood three feet from his position. The effect split the trunk horizontally in the jagged, broken pattern of an earthquake fault line, bringing the maple down to the ground in a matter of moments.

Once Charon had regained himself, he scanned around to see if there were any mortals who had seen the outburst.

There were none.

And then, as if they had been with him all along, the images of Thanatos and Hypnos appeared in his thoughts. They spoke to him.

Hypnos:

"Easy, brother. Rest your mind for now, for soon the one you came for will come, following after these two like a starving animal caught on the scent of an easy meal. And then-"

Thanatos:

"You will deliver once again the gift I give to all mortals, the one I have always trusted you as the final arbiter of its deliverance."

Their visages smiled at him, then vanished.

That yawning chasm, that void must always remain, for that is how one allows those lost in times gone by to return to us, even if for only a fleeting, brief moment, thought Charon.

Brothers.

Charon's heart had never stopped aching to see their faces, even if it were but for one last time.

As Andreas approached the (*stoplight*), that infernal word he'd already twice heard in his head resurfaced yet again. This time however, it did not appear in his thoughts like the blinding glimmer of the midday sun.. The intensity of its momentary flash would sear the retinas that caught sight of it, leaving behind an altered perception of color as a visual, albeit temporary echo. This effect was just the shadow of the reflected sunlight trapped within the relative darkness of one's mind. But that distortion of a person's vision would never last long; eyesight returning to normal within minutes.

The previous two times that word came to Andreas, its dynamic matched that of this glimmer – the memory of what the word was and its significance had dissipated into the darkness of disremembering within mere moments.

But on this third occasion, the word did no such thing. Instead, it repeated, over and over and over, rendering clear thought impossible in seconds.

ARSENIKOSARSENIKOSARSENIKOSARSENIKOS ARSENIKOSARSENIKOSARSENI-

- Andreas finally brought the car to a complete stop, he could hear nothing else but the word being shouted within himself, from a hundred different shadowed corners throughout not only his mind, but what felt like his spirit as well. He...

Andreas**ARSENIKOS**

(murderer)

...felt panic at that instant, followed by the freezing grip of true fear. This kind of fear was paralyzing, turning every muscle to stone and every drop of blood to syrup. It was the kind that prey feels when it finds itself trapped; unable to move as a predator bears down on upon it.

He thought then that if he didn't make it to the *(funeral parlor)*, find the two brothers, and possess the coins within the next few minutes, his psyche would shatter completely and his quest would be lost.

He put his head down on the *(steering wheel)* and closed his eyes, taking advantage of the circumstances to try and summon enough strength to continue.

His respite was then cut short by the jarring sound of a car behind him blasting its signal *(horn)* –

blasting its horn to spur him on his way. Andreas looked up and saw the light machine had illuminated the bottom lamp a green color, allowing him to

76

continue on to his destination. The person driving the vehicle behind him must share a similar urgency-

ARSENIKOSyouwouldnevertoleratesuchan

insult**ARSENIKOS**openhisthroatoutwithyour

bladelikealloftheothers**ARSENIKOS**

-to complete its journey as he had.

Andreas turned the vehicle left onto the road that brought travelers onto the funeral home property.

He brought the vehicle to a stop, a few feet from the path that lead to the buildings' front door.

**ARSENIKOSARSENIKOSARSENIKOS
ARSENIKOSARSENIKOSARSENIKOS
ARSENIKOSARSENIKOSARSENIKOS
ARSENIKOSARSENIKOSARSENIKOS
ARSENIKOSARSENIKOSARSENIKOS**

He exited the car, and staggered towards the building. The world was a whirlwind. He could no longer make out distinct shapes. All was a blur.

**ARSENIKOSARSENIKOSARSENIKOS
ARSENIKOSARSENIKOSARSENIKOS
ARSENIKOSARSENIKOSARSENIKOS
ARSENIKOSARSENIKOSARSENIKOS
ARSENIKOSARSENIKOSARSENIKOS**

Andreas somehow reached the door, and fumbled at it as a blind man would have, eventually finding the knob. He pushed it open and staggered inside.

He weakly called out inside the reception area.

"I am looking for the brothers? My name is...my name is Andreas and I..."

But he could not finish the sentence. The world spun into darkness. The last thing he experienced was the left side of his face striking the ground with a crack.

A dream, then. Presented as a tragedy in three acts:

Ο θάνατος του Αρσενικού

"The Death of Arsenikos"

He found himself in a darkened area, dimly lit with just the light that found its way into the space through two tiny, grime covered windows. It was just enough to be able to discern that the room he was in was filthy.

Appallingly filthy.

The ground was covered with the rotted forms of almost everything that could and would be found in a living area; wood, discarded, half-eaten meals, even the bones of victims, their flesh long since non-existent, all blackened and brittle from exposure to the fetid air within. The home of someone poor and destitute – and deranged. The l"ess fortunate" existed in the great city of Mycenae, despite its wealth and standing among the other municipalities of Greece, in the corners and crevasses where the common citizenry dared not venture.

But Mycenae wasn't his home. He couldn't remember where it had been he spent his youth, exactly. But he had come here because of the wealth of Mycenae, and the relative weakness of its citizens.

Their men.

Their women.

Especially the loathsome and polluted animals that passed for women here. They all needed to be put down. But before that – there was a lesson.

In this vision, three women were bound to a concrete wall with chains that held their arms above their heads. They were triplets – identical in every way. An absolute abomination, that the so-called gods could allow such a thing to happen. Upon seeing them for the first time in one of the marketplaces, he nearly vomited at the sight of them. They could not be allowed to exist for a day longer than he could help it. Their parents likely thought them a gift from Aphrodite, Athena, or one of the other immortal whores. Deluded souls.

Now, they were reduced to what they were. Filthy animals.

All three sobbed, wept, and cried. Pathetic.

He drew close to them, feeling both excitement and anticipation at what would come next. It was the only thing he loved about being alive, those fullest of moments when every fiber of his being, every pound of flesh was charged with undiluted, raw power. It crashed through him like a tidal wave, the crest appearing the second he made eye contact with the next soul he'd send to the underworld.

When his face came close to the first of them, he became aware of a covering upon his face. He touched it in a few spots, and was reminded of its soft texture. Smooth, and satisfying...

It was his mask.

How could he have forgotten it? Just the symbolic significance alone made it such that he of all people should forget it. He who had crafted that facial covering - as both a symbol and a warning - should never be seen by others without it, let alone those pigs he brought into his home.

It restored him.

He'd fashioned it from flesh taken from the remains of the very first life that he took. The one life he'd thought would seal the abyss within him, the abyss that plagues his thoughts in every waking moment, the abyss that...*ate at him* forever.

His father had been alive for the duration as he'd peeled the skin from his face with nothing but the dull edge of a rock he'd found in the road. He could still hear the old man's agonized screams as the stone took five, six, even seven passes to separate

81

flesh away from his skull. Eventually, it came away, and became the mask he wore while he performed his work.

And the abyss? The void? The...nothing within? It never filled.

It only grew larger, and larger in the middle of him.

When he felt that emptiness once again, the dream felt more like reality. Certainly more real than what the world had turned into since he had since made his own journey into the realms of death, the underworld.

What lesson shall be delivered today? He had a special inspiration. Three identical women turned into a puzzle, a kind of game that would be impossible to solve.

Or win.

He started with their feet, making six cuts at different heights off the ankle for each and continued in this way for every part of them. Of course, he would tie off his amputations, his pieces of each. Whereas these sisters would serve more as a lesson for the world, for the gods, he thought they should be allowed to at least attempt to learn as well. He doubted their ability to truly understand his wisdom.

As the ultimate measure of life ran out from the last of the three still living, he was drawn back to his earlier thoughts upon his own death. His own journey to the underworld.

How had that happened? How had he-

But it was still a dream, so the image of the three helpless women was replaced by one that stood in diametrically opposite relation.

The door to this rancid, festering pit of a dwelling is smashed open, the light of midday pouring in from the now ajar entryway to his domain.

Through it had come Spartans – seven of them.

Tisamenus, King of Sparta, Mycenae, and Argos had sent these men after him. Maybe a few days prior and certainly not in time to save the triplets. Tisamenus must have calculated carefully, knowing that he'd need seven of his most bloodthirsty soldiers to be sure they'd at least ensure he'd never leave his home alive. Killing him would likely take seven of them to finally end his life, for

he was terror. HE was the God of Death, and not some made up persona in a fable to disguise the truth from the people: the truth that there were no gods on Olympus or in Hades, only he, the bringer of sorrow.

Their captain, the first through the door and also the first to catch a glimpse of what remained of the three captive girls, almost dropped his spear at sight of them. He'd made the mistake of looking into the corner where they had once been chained.

They had been cut up into fifty, maybe even a hundred parts, each consisting of varying sections of their anatomy... and he had been quite successful in producing an inventory with no order or consistency to the items therein. He'd fashioned them into an obscene jumble of puzzle pieces, to which there was never any possibility of reassembling them – even if doing so meant they could be brought back to life from their horrific fates.

He shouted out his name:

"ARSENIKOS!!!"

Not an actual name...but this pleased him, for it felt as if he was being worshiped. He was no longer just a man. He was everything a man should be.

"And who are you, one who has come to worship at my feet?"

"Who am I, asks the twisted offspring of a cursed mother and an insane father? I am... *ANDREAS OF*

84

SPARTA... and I shall be the man who captured the creature!!"

Arsenikos merely laughed at the man.

"A wonderful name! One day I shall use it and take more lives in all of its false meaning. Then, no one shall be able to tell the difference between you or I! Such as it should be," Arsenikos proclaimed, the remaining Spartans circling him.

"Since all of you boy-fucking Spartans are so proud of your sanctioned murdering. I think that I shall change it, however. Make it...my own, somehow. I'll change it instead to Andreas of Mycen..."

There was a thud and a brief interlude of darkness.

The final act:

It begins with the full, blinding power of the midday sun, outside, and within his home. The soldiers had not killed him then and there in his sanctum of obscenity and violence. They had taken him alive.

They had brought him before Tisamenus, and Tisamenus decided upon the location and the means of his execution. They had brought him there the very next afternoon.

He lay, flat on his back, face pointed straight to the sky, such as he would when he lay upon the shores of the River Styx. Each of his limbs had been immobilized, his wrists and ankles tied down by four tightened lengths of rope secured to stakes driven deep into the earth.

Arsenikos thought of the words of Heraclitus, who mused that one cannot step into the same river twice. And yet, here he was, restored to himself once again, through the power of remembrance of what and who once was. To be fair, he had never stepped into any river at any point. His worthless musings may still have some value to the rest of the half-wits and the weak-willed.

Despite there not being true 'sound' within the confines of a dream-state, at least not in the strictest definition, Arsenikos could hear his executioners all around him, their numbers in the hundreds at a minimum.

Similarly, Arsenikos could not truly smell or feel the sticky, sugary substance with which his entire body had been coated. But since this scene was another replay of a lost, albeit final, memory from his life, Arsenikos knew it was the sweet nectar of the finest honeys produced by the merchants of Mycenae.

Within moments, the first vanguards from each of the several species of insects that would come to feast upon him would arrive.

Arsenikos felt an almost hysterical kind of glee with the knowledge that despite experiencing their death sentence a second time, he was doing so having escaped the inferno...as well as not actually having to feel the hundreds upon hundreds and then thousands of stings, bites, egg-layings of all the vermin that resided in the field he died in centuries before.

The citizenry of the city-states under Tisamenus' rule bestowed upon him his name, Arsenikos, which merely

meant 'masculine, male', for they had no other description of him other than that he was male. This was good; he had restored himself from the indignities he'd suffered at the hands of his mother and father.

What a wonderful dream. Soothing, even. He could feel his flesh slowly, painlessly being devoured as he recalled them all. Hundreds of them, their souls sent on to the underworld. How many of his victims had Lord Charon ferried across Styx to the

Elysian Fields because they had been murdered? Had they lived their lives out, these fools likely would have made years upon years of queestionable decisions, carried out morally indefensible actions and thus relegated themselves to Hades or worse.

Arsenikos considered himself a hero in such a fashion.

The dream at last faded, meaning that Arsenikos had begun waking back into the world he'd stolen away into. How long had it taken for his first life to finally end in that field, he'd asked himself before he swam up and away from the vision.

Ah yes, he thought, having remembered.

Six full days of their torture, but even that level of conviction was not enough to put a final, eternal end to his work. For now, it would continue and then? He would still be able to enter into the same eternal afterlife as those who'd lived their so-called "good" lives...

Their father's condo wasn't visible from the circular road that encompassed the eight-building complex he'd lived in. Six of the eight formed the outer perimeter of structures, and two of them were built within the interior they formed.

On the exterior side of that road, the town forest acted as ample buffer to the development and gave it a natural - and expensive - seclusion. The company that had built the condos used this specific feature as both a selling point and a justification for gouging the shit out of each condominium's listings. They carried that strategy further by making the two buildings in the center of the development the most expensive. Stavros Poulos made the kind of money that allowed him to easily afford one of those two, and thus forced any visitors, guests, or deliveries to perform a bit more pathfinding to find his home than just relying upon a GPS.

Chris had visited his father several times since he'd moved there following his divorce from their mother three years prior.

Dante, on the other hand, had no clue which place belonged to his father and couldn't help but start asking questions.

"So what, he picked the one which mom would never be able to find? Isolated himself in a hole in the woods hidden by houses all around him?"

"He got one of the two most expensive ones, Dante. Because - "

"Was a joke, Chris."

"Let me finish man. He picked this complex because the man had no fucking idea how to meet new people, how to start over. The people moving in here are all from his demo."

"His what?"

"Demographic. Late forties to fifties, divorced, all trying to land on their feet and all with the bank account balance to do so comfortably. Dad used his real estate skills to find a place where he wouldn't..."

Chris tailed off in his by-the-numbers rundown of how their father came to live in this tucked-away suburban spot. And Dante, for his part, seemed to notice something was off with Chris a moment or two before it occurred.

"Yo. Chris. *Christos.*" Dante looked over at him and saw him stopped in his tracks a couple steps behind and staring straight ahead. Dante waved a hand in front of his face to snap Chris back to reality.

"Hey. Zippahhead," he said as he waved.

Or maybe it was the name-calling that did it.

"What? Hunh? Oh shit, sorry. Got like, this weird vertigo dude. The fuck was I saying?"

"You were about to tell me, not using real estate bullshit, why Dad picked this spinoff of *The Stepford Wives* to separate from ma."

"Yeah. Mom. Anyway." They continued on.

It hadn't ended well between their parents. Stavros and Alyssa Poulos were the textbook marriage between people who stay together *for the sake of the kids*. So, as the years rolled past, they'd cultivated and curated resentment, bitterness, and a barely contained hostility as if they were branches on a kind of grotesque Bonsai tree. An *anti*-Bonsai tree. By the time they'd actually filed papers to call it quits, each had reached that point where both Stavros and Alyssa made no secret to either that they'd each begun their own extra-marital affairs.

"That dude Rick didn't stay for the reception. *Did he stay for the reception?*"

"No, Dante. He did not, thankfully. It was awkward as shit that he was there for mass, and everyone there felt it."

"Why awkward? So what if him and Dad hated each other? Just because Mom's been gone for a couple of years didn't mean he just stopped talking to me... bro he was there because of..."

"Yeah. There it is," Chris motioned towards their father's front door.

Dante put his hand on his brother's shoulder to stop him from continuing. "Wait – that's it, isn't it?"

"What are you talking about Dante? I just want to..."

"No man. You give me all kinds of shit about not talking to Dad for fucking years, but you don't even have the balls to even for a second consider that maybe I had a good reason for not talking to him."

"You completely shut him the fuck out, Dante. You broke his heart."

"Oh yeah buddy? Newsflash, Christos. I *did* try to contact him. A bunch of times in the past year. Never picked up the phone, never returned a message. I figured after Mom died..."

Chris spun around and shot Dante the hurt look this time around.

Dante stopped short. He could see his younger brother getting caught up in his emotions like he was apt to do - like their father did as well. Chris would short circuit so quickly and so badly that for the first time it became clear to Dante exactly *why* it was that Chris had to hold so tightly onto his routine and ambition and the next task on the daily planner.

Because once the kid had lost his grip , it was too much for him to just get it back. He skidded right out of control.

"Never mind, man. Let's just get it done," Dante finished.

The two of them then strode shoulder-to-shoulder towards the building. Dante turned the doorknob – unlocked.

He looked to Chris with a look of both puzzlement and alarm. Chris reassured him.

"I requested they leave it unlocked. Don't have a key, and I didn't feel like co-ordinating with management to have them meet us here. Privacy and all that."

"Always thinking, Christos, always thinking."

Dante pushed open the front door and the two of them entered the foyer of. what used to be their fathers' home.

Arsenikos opened his eyes and was met with a sharp, throbbing pain that originated from one side of his skull reverberated against the opposite, and continued this movement without even the slightest hint of ever diminishing.

However, its sheer intensity brought him to full awareness far faster than if he hadn't struck his face upon the ground when he'd lost consciousness.... 'twas a double-edged floor, so to speak.

He tilted his head upward at a slight angle and scanned his surroundings to take measure of what had occurred while he was out cold.

He could tell immediately that he'd been moved, as a quick survey revealed that the room he'd awoken in was far different than the one where he'd first entered the building.

There were steel implements he did not recognize laid out upon a pale green cloth in an organized fashion. Near these implements, their individual functions a mystery to him at the moment, were a series of bottles of thick fluids of varying colors. One was labeled "METASYN", its contents a viscous yellow-orange tint. Just next to that was a container that held an unnatural substance of pumice green.

Whatever was carried out in this area, it was done away from the prying eyes of the common citizen. And whomever did their work here knew death as if it were a trusted friend.

As if to confirm this, Arsenikos then detected that the room's general aroma didn't just carry a hint, but rather was so permeated with the sweet yet rancid odors of death, decay, decomposition, and rot, the air itself felt heavy, suffocating. Arsenikos was certain that burning every wall, window, beam and board with flames brought forth by oil would neither purify nor purge the smell from the building's smoldering remains. Odors and smells were always such powerful triggers of memory, and this repulsive stench brought back the most familiar and cherished of all...

It reminded him of home.

His pit. Where he had once told a Spartan he would take his name and murder using it. He smiled.

I keep my promises, Andrea the Spartan, thought the man who'd only just recalled his true name but had thought himself Andreas of Mycenae minutes before, having revisited this memory moments earlier in those first parts of his dream.

This could be no coincidence, then.

He grinned. It was all meant to be.

Arsenikos decided that he must know what this menagerie of metal tools were at once - above all else, he felt right within himself and his surroundings for the first time in what felt like centuries, yet these *promising* creations remained alien to him.

Why was this so? All the collective knowledge of his fellow mortals had poured into him, wanted or unwanted. It made no sense.

Then, a thought:

You don't have to return to the Underworld when you take the coins from the brothers. This place could be yours.

Arsenikos has returned.

He sat bolt upright, and in doing so a wave of vertigo and dizziness overtook him. The room began to spin, so much so that Arsenikos felt for an instant that he might vomit. And, before this disorientation could subside he heard a voice call out from somewhere behind him.

"Mr. Andreas! Good heavens, man! Please lay back down. You've taken a terrible fall."

Arsenikos glanced to his left, then his right in a confused and ultimately vain attempt to locate the source of the voice. The man who had just spoken then materialized at the precise moment when Arsenikos' head returned to its natural position.

This minor occurrence infuriated Arsenikos. He assumed that the man, despite having lifted him from the floor near the entrance of the building and making him comfortable here in this room, was showing disrespect by seeming to play a truncated round of peek-a-boo with him.

"Who are you? Where am I?" asked Arsenikos, faking a higher level of confusion than his mind actually resided in at that instant.

"Dunsmuir, Nathaniel Dunsmuir, sir," the tall man said as he extended a hand towards Arsenikos.

"They call me Ar- uh, Andreas," he stuttered in response. He smiled back with the practiced amiability of a psychopath with an endless supply of masks to choose from.

"Ah, my mistake, sir. I assumed your last name was Andreas. Forgive me for asking you while you're in such a state, but what is your business here, today, at this time? We don't have another..."

Arsenikos had stopped listening to this withered, babbling idiot the second he started speaking again.

Instead, once he was certain that he could stand without falling to the ground once again, he moved towards the shining implements that had captivated his attention almost since he had awoken.

Arsenikos then cut Dunsmuir off from polluting the air any further with his nonsense.

"What *is* this place, Dunsmuir? What are...these?" Arsenikos picked one of the implements up, a cylinder-shaped object that had been fitted with a six-inch needle at one end and two holes, made with steel, that appeared to be crafted for fingers to be placed within.

Dunsmuir appeared genuinely baffled by the question. Did this man even know where he was? Didn't he know what an embalming room was?

"Uh, that's a connecting syringe, Andreas. We use that particular one to ensure the areas of the deceased are properly filled with the correct preservation fluid."

"Preservation?"

"Yes, sir. So as to prevent any further decay of the body long enough to last beyond the funeral rites."

Arsenikos put his fingers through the holes and in doing so, accidentally squirted a bright yellow fluid from a needle. He was delighted with both the idea of being able to preserve one of *his* playthings indefinitely and the operation of this... syringe.

Dunsmuir, in the meantime, had run out of patience.

"Andreas, if you'd just answer my question I- "

"I'm looking for my nephews. They told me they were coming here and I'd planned on meeting them."

"Oh. OH!" Dunsmuir was relieved by his answer. This man had no viable reason to be here at his business and Dunsmuir had instinctively begun to grow suspicious of him – regardless of the accident he'd suffered.

"Oh dear heavens, man, why didn't you say so? Chris and Dante were both just here. Why don't we both just head over to my office and we can get some more information, and before we forget let's call you an ambulance and get you taken care of, hey?"

Office. Information. Chris. Dante.

And this man was intent on calling some kind of medical servants to this house.

Which meant more officers.

Dunsmuir had simultaneously exhausted his usefulness and presented himself as both an obstacle and a threat.

99

"I don't think so."

And with a movement faster than winter lightning, with more power than a thousand tyrants, and with more precision than the movement of the sun through the sky, Arsenikos plunged the connecting syringe so deep into Dunsmuir's right eye the needle penetrated that point of the cerebellum that sits adjacent to the brainstem.

Dunsmuir slowly and smoothly dropped to the ground. Dunsmuir's face had frozen not in a face of fear, but in the exact countenance he held as he uttered the last words of his life.

Before Dunsmuir could reach it however, Arsenikos pushed that part of the syringe that made the bright yellow fluid erupt from the needle – in the same manner as he had when he'd stuck the weapon into his skull.

There had been so much of this potion in it that it had first welled up in the entry wound socket, and then overflowing that cavity such that Dunsmuir would die with three rivulets of embalming fluid making their way across his face.

Arsenikos considered for a moment turning Dunsmuir's face into a new mask for himself, but alas there was no time.

One of the brothers, then. He'd wear it when, and if, one day he returned to the underworld to give the ferryman his due.

If.

"

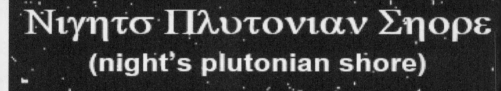

Νιγητσ Πλυτονιαν Σηορε

(night's plutonian shore)

Once Charon regained himself after splitting the tree, he intently watched the brothers the rest of their way as they walked to the dwelling where Stavros, their father had lived for his final years. He took special note of one moment -when it appeared as if Christos was going to faint. It proved to be nothing more a small bout of vertigo, yet it had reminded Charon of something peculiar about the boy.

Just a few decades before this day, he'd become aware of the creation of Christos and Dante's souls. Dante had been forty-two years prior, Christos thirty-three. This part, of course, was nothing unusual, as Charon was always aware whenever a new soul began their journey; as with each and every mortal that had ever existed. In the time it took the two of them to traverse the distance from their conveyance to the house, seven hundred and twelve more had come into existence.

The world had changed, evolved, and new cultures and gods emerged. Charon could still sense where souls would have gone, were they all still devoted to those of the ancient Greeks. Belief always had been, and forever would be the primary frequency by which that eternal part of a mortal's being would vibrate along. Charon had surmised, long ago, that the songs may change, but the chords would always remain the same.

Were the plane of the living still as connected to Charon's as it had been millennia before, six hundred and eighty-eight of those souls would have passed onto Hades to spend the rest of eternity. The small minority that were left over would have been destined for either the greater rewards found in the Elysian Fields, or condemned to the prisons and torture of Tartarus. Where they belonged.

Charon noted that Dante, like his father before him, was one of that cluster of mortals whose fate lay waiting for them in the Fields. There were bloodlines that persisted, even to this day, of the genuine and the good of heart and intention. The stories of their lives rarely bore this out, as the world tended to chew them up as if they were delicacies – this much would never change.

Lord Charon sensed Stavros' presence there, waiting for his boys with both infinite patience and infinite love. It was clear then to Charon that Stavros had re-connected his soul to the old ways of his culture for that exact reason. To make a place for himself and his boys.

But when Charon reached out to Chris...there was nothing. No promise of a serene, peaceful, pain-free future. No forthcoming damnation to experience the very worst things in all of existence. Not even as yet another subject under the yoke of immortality's asshole himself – Hades.

Something was wrong. Different. Here in Christos Poulos was a mortal who stood outside the eternal continuum, had been separated from all others as if for a purpose the likes of which had never existed before.

Charon had never felt a soul such as the one that Chris possessed, and yet the person he had just been in the presence of - albeit briefly - felt as familar as an old friend, a lost love, or a...

but Lord Charon could not finish the thought.

He was near.

And he had just killed again. Three times, in fact. Within the span of just two hours. The third time just minutes before.

Charon emerged from his nest to position himself better to meet his quarry.

This beast, this twisted mongrel, this abhorrence in the shape of a mortal must not be allowed to continue existing anywhere else other than within Kronos' jaw – where his mind and spirit would be forever devoured by the mad father of the Titans.

Lord Charon intended on sending him there.

"Arsenikos", they had called him. The combined citizenry of three city states had lived in such abject terror – a fear so deep it could cause actual physical pain – his true name was lost to the shadows of irrelevance cast by the truth of the man.

(serial killer)

(demon)

(the first)

The sky grew dark.

And then, borne through the darkness by the twin lamps at the front of his conveyance came the monster. Hades had warned him, that should he remember who he once was, Charon alone may not be enough to match his sheer malevolence.

He would have to be.

Charon closed in as Arsenikos brought his vehicle to a stop...

106

...and called out to him by his true name, the one Arsenikos hadn't heard since he was a fourteen-year old child.

The one his mother had cried out in horror and agony as he took her life from her. She had been his second, after his father.

Arsenikos whispered under his breath:

"The ferryman."

So Lord Charon had come for Arsenikos himself. Perhaps Hades had sent him, perhaps not. It made no difference which was the case. Charon had always possessed the power to kill any or all of the gods on Olympus and elsewhere, and yet never had. Instead, this supposed higher being had willingly chosen to be their errand boy, fetching this soul, guiding that one along, returning still another to its assigned seating in the life that followed.

At the prospect of killing such a tedious demigod, Arsenikos felt such a powerful current of pure elation he feared for an instant he may lose consciousness yet again.

Strangely, he then saw a series of words, each made up of sequences of letters that suggested associations with at least two or more of the sciences. He knew what they all were meant to represent when listed together as they had been in his thoughts – these were the invisible ingredients of the aforementioned elation. His knowledge kept growing minutes by minute.

The people of this day and age appeared and deliberately carried themselves as dim-witted morons, as if ignorance was the most desirable characteristic for a citizen to possess and exhibit. And yet – the advances in technology he'd seen in just over an hour were staggering.

One would have to be as stupid as they not to realize that the intelligence required to invent such things had invented the things that would ultimately wipe its presence from humanity.

Arsenikos was in no need of such frivolity in this moment. No need of silly, hand-held *guns* - once again, a tool of this day and age that imparted a sense or feeling of power to those that carried them while clearly demonstrating they had none to speak of.

Instead, Arsenikos had jammed semilunar needles of varying lengths under each of his fingernails – fashioning himself a set of oddly shaped, makeshift yet still viciously cruel-looking, stainless steel claws. In his left hand, he brandished an almost identical syringe to the one he'd used to murder Dunsmuir earlier. Arsenikos had filled this one with a creamy, bright green fluid that had no business being in the presence of anyone not directly experienced with its use. It was comprised of a combination of chemicals Arsenikos knew to be by far and away the most violently toxic to life. This foul substance, found amongst Dunsmuir's collection of poisons and potions intended to preserve death would instead serve a purpose converse to intended use.

And lastly, in his right, he held an unholy three-foot long steel catheter razor-sharpened at its terminus.

He'd spun around on Charon before the decrepit, powerless not-god could manage to even swing either of his feeble *sagaris* at him, let alone land a blow. sink either of his sharpened hammers into Arsenikos.

Moreover, Charon had moved far slower in this current sequence of events than he ever had in the entirety of his existence.

Arsenikos plunged the catheter into Charon's belly before Charon had even a fraction of a second to counter.

He thought:

How...?

"Why Lord Charon. How embarrassing. Were it not for those ridiculous goggles upon your face, I could savor the look of pure shock in your eyes at having been bested by...*a mere mortal.*"

Arsenikos began to laugh hysterically.

"It appears that time has finally has gotten the best of the 'Lord of Death'," he gloated.

And at that, Lord Charon took his turn at a smile. It was bittersweet, for at that moment he longed so greatly that his older brother was present then to hear Charon speak his response.

"You have me mistaken for someone else, *mere mortal.* Thanatos gifted me my *sagaris* to grant me just a fraction of his power...over *death.*"

"Arsenikos...when Kronos was cast down and rendered powerless, the one who would take his mantle was chosen from the sons of Erebos. And so...

...in his place, *I was chosen as the god of...*"

At the instant before he spoke the word, it had frozen all around Charon. It took an incalculable amount of effort to hold the universe still in such a way, so he moved as quickly as he could.

He stepped back from Arsenikos enough to then extract the steel rod from his lower torso.

Mighty Charon held all of existence at a stand-still while enduring pure agony.

None but the very highest of immortals in all the pantheons and in all the cosmos would hear Charon.

For at the sound of his wailing, the ones that did hear him were reminded of how each, every, and all feared Charon...

...and loved him as well.

For Lord Charon had chosen his role among the gods and goddesses, the titans, and his own ancient family simply for the sole reason that for all their combined power, all their pomposity and grandeur and ego to separate the worlds of the living and the dead for eternity. Any of them could have taken this charge, but only the lord of time as experienced by the individual, and not that nebulous quantity with its clocks and its measurements.

112

Why he had done this, none of them could say. But were one to ask him for the answer, he would tell you, openly, without reservation. Why he had chosen to ferry the souls of the living to the underworld for eternity.

Not one being in all of creation could give him his brothers back to him.

Their domains were sleep and death, and as such once they'd taken their mantles vanished into both.

Thanatos was not a death-bringer, far from it in fact. All he ever wanted to do laugh, and make others laugh in turn. His was the state of death, the absence of life. To prove this, his weapons, the *sagaris*, he used to bring those that deserved it the chance to live again.

Thanatos had been taken from him by fate.

And Hypnos? The hyperactive Hypnos, never sleeping, always with ideas and schemes and plans. His imagination never ceased, never stopped, not for a second. Hypnos would drive he and Thanatos mad sometimes.

And from his eternal slumber, he gives the world their dreams, selflessly, wordlessly, forever.

Charon no longer cared about any of that. He wanted his brothers by his side again.

Time passes differently for and among the broken-hearted. Days and weeks slip by unnoticed. Seconds and minutes stretch into infinities. Lord Charon had long since forgotten what those words even meant – if they ever had any real meaning at all.

But on this one occasion, an occurrence which had never in all of the vast, endless depths of time.

A mortal would hear his cry.

It still made no sense to Chris. The coins, Dunsmuir's story, Dante's outburst...none of it.

And to most people like Chris, the order to which they set their lives and the rules they believed that in abiding by them, they'd not only live their best possible lives but also be the best version of themselves to others tended to make them more vulnerable to the disruptive nature of things that didn't make sense.

But for Chris in particular, the things he couldn't make sense of sat in his thoughts like a fraying wire somewhere in the walls of a large house. Within a few moments, the frayed, exposed part of that wire would begin to spark and crackle with electricity.

Nothing would be done about it, since it wasn't like something as minor as a little exposed metal cause any actual, significant structural damage to Chris' metaphorical thought-house. Moreover, it was easily pushed aside at the moment it began to spark – it'll stop, eventually.

It never did, however.

So by the time Chris had finished sorting through his father's office desk drawers, his thought-house was already a total loss; a smouldering disaster in which three firemen had tragically lost their lives attempting to douse the flames.

"Alright, everybody out of the pool," Chris announced to an empty room. He marched across the office to the room adjacent, the kitchen, before continuing on to pinpoint his brother's exact location.

Dante was in the only bedroom when Chris stormed in. Dante was sitting on top of the solid blue duvet cover that their father had likely made the very first day he'd moved in to the condo complex - and had remained undisturbed ever since. Their father had been a notoroius couch-sleeper.

Chris did not *slam* the door closed per se, but rather, exerted enough force on it to...extra close it.

"Yo."

Chris sounded as if he'd just launched his new Hip Hop career just thirty seconds before entering.

Dante looked up from a thick, large book bound with a kind of foam substance that bore the kind of sour milk color that gave its game up as a photo album from the late 1970s.

"Hi?"

"Listen man, you gotta expl..." Chris stopped short, alarmed and frightened into silence by what

117

had started happening – or rather, stopped happening altogether.

Halfway through enunciating the word 'explain' Chris' surroundings, as well as his older brother appeared as if they'd all been part of a state-of-the-art virtual reality video game simulation that someone had hit the pause button to go to the bathroom or something to eat.

Dante was the most disarming aspect of this...effect? A glitch in the matrix? Chris thought that it might be resulting from the sudden onset of a serious medical condition within either his brain or central nervous system.

Chris did not have to worry about that possibility for more than one or two seconds, for then came the most anguished, tortured scream he had ever heard in his entire life. It lasted just a few seconds, but while it was being let out, seemingly from a creature whose lungs were the size of a planet it felt interminable.

A wail that loud in any other circumstance would easily have a hundred percent chance of inflicting permanent hearing loss with but a nanosecond of exposure to its sheer volume.

But Chris hadn't felt so much as a tiny twinge of mild discomfort. Before he could think to leave the broken VR game he found himself within and go in search of whomever or whatever had been injured so badly that only calling the almighty himself to remedy the situation would suffice, the scream fell quiet and someone on the outside of the VR world had kicked the console it began working again.

Dante blinked. Chris saw this and asked him if he was okay.

Dante looked twice as confused as when Chris inquired as to his well-being, because to him it was more than a bit strange that in one instant, Chris looked like he was ready to finally throw down with him and in the next appeared ready to perform CPR or first aid on him.

"Are you okay, man? Came in here a second ago ready to knock me the fuck out about something. What's uh...what's going on?"

Chris considered this question for less than a second before (correctly) deducing that from his brother's perspective, nothing out of an episode of Doctor Who occurred.

Furthermore, he hadn't heard the sound made when a Great Old One stubbed his big toe on hell while walking amongst the dimensions of reality, either. Chris concluded at that moment that he would never, for the remainder of his days, ever forget that sound.

Smartly, Chris pivoted back to the instant he'd walked into the room, irate and looking for some answers, goddamnit.

"Dante. You and Dad don't speak for literally years. In all that while, I'm stuck in between you two assholes as a designated carrier pigeon. Incredibly fair, and not at all a constant source of misery."

"But then, Dunsmuir starts talking about made-up myths and legends, coins and crossing the river Styx, and you launch out of your fuckin chair defending Dad's latest brand of insanity tooth and nail. I mean, what the fuck, Dante? How the hell did - *when* the hell did you know about all of this?"

Dante, whose mouth was fully agape by the time Chris had finished, arose from the bed. He sighed and then snickered to himself.

"This shit's been driving you batshit since we left Morningside, hasn't it buckaroo?"

"Just answer the q-"

"I *never* knew, ya big friggn dope. Not once. At no time did he ever mentiion any of it, because he wasn't stupid, bro. If he came to either of us and said he'd adopted Poseidon, Lord of the Oceans as his Lord and Saviour, we'd have the guy committed."

Dante's answer only seemed to piss Chris off further.

"You think Dad would have wanted you to be the one defending his character, or his judgement, in ensuring that he'd been buried with whatever – the first bronze coins ever made seven million years ago so a fake guy on a fake boat will take him to a fake promised land?"

Dante stood up at this last, now officially upset.

"Yes. A thousand percent."

Chris scoffed.

"Chris, a few fucking hours ago, you show up at my place and call it a demilitarized zone. You come inside, and you're a complete prick to a girl you don't even know and rush her out the door. After continuing to be a total cock for the remaining time I'm getting ready, you let up just enough for me to catch my breath. Thanks bud. You're the best. Then I ask how long the drive is, and you lose your mind again. Sorry I didn't know the fuckin' town Dad lived in, Chris. It's not like I have a car to drive there anyway."

"Aren't you even in the slightest bit upset or sad you missed out on that time with him, Dante? You're never going to be able to get that back."

Dante gently pushed his brother aside and made to leave their fathers' bedroom – and Chris – behind.

Before he could depart the room completely, however, Dante turned back to his brother to leave one last piece of truth with him.

"But all those all other years we *did* have each other? All thirty-four of them?"

"No one will ever be able to take them away from me, either. You can't live your life with an idea in your head that you can end all of your relationships with loved ones on good notes. Death comes for us all, and sometimes it's boring, sometimes it's a case of some seriously shitty luck, and sometimes it's so batshit crazy believing it happened the way it did seems even more batshit crazy than the actual dying."

"So what the fuck Dante? Just...don't try?"

"No man, no." Dante sighed.

"The truth, Chris? We're lucky, REALLY fucking lucky, if we stick the landing on four, maybe five of those people we're close to. The rest will always have coulda woulda shouldas tailing behind them like those tin cans on the back of *Just Married* vehicles when they leave the church. The happy couple looks beautiful as they drive off and vanish into the distance, but there's these loud, dented cans

122

dragging on the street, adding the sound of literal fucking trash to an otherwise beautiful scene. Me beating myself up for making the stand I did with Dad? Not gonna happen. Me attaching that kind of guilt to doing and saying what I believe in? No. Fucking. Way. Do you know what's left after each person *that* close to you dies?"

"No, Dante, what?"

"You'll figure it out eventually. And when you do? You'll stop all this shit with perfecting everything with the people you care most about. You'll start accepting shit for what it is, and you'll be happier for it. You know what little brother? Come to think of it, I think I'm going to find that girl Violet's num-"

Chris dropped to one knee as if the utterance of Violet's name had the additional effect of punching him directly in the balls.

And although Chris' eyes remained wide open, all he saw was a parking lot not far from Chris' apartment.

Police flashers were everywhere. Plainclothes and uniformed officers stood around a body - a murder victim – on the ground. Chris' mind's eye zoomed in again to the victim.

Violet. Her head had been entirely caved in on one side. She'd been murdered within minutes of leaving Dante's apartment.

Dante must have noticed something on his brothers' face. There was something fucking weird going on with him, and Dante grew increasingly more worried about him by the moment.

"Chris. The hell is going on with you dude?"

Chris stood up, keeping his face pointed downward towards the floor.

"CHRIS."

Chris finally turned his face upwards from the ground and faced his brother. Dante saw that in the time he'd spent down on one knee, Chris had been crying like had when they were kids.

Chris' entire face glistened with tears, the salty, clear liquid catching the light from his fathers' bedroom behind him in such a way as to impart an distinct, glowing quality to it.

"Violet's dead, Dante."

"What?"

"Violet's fucking dead, Dante! Somebody caved the side of her skull in with their bare hands and she's fucking dead *and it's my fucking fault!!!*"

Dante extended his left arm and grasped his brother's right shoulder in an attempt to comfort him. It failed. Instead, Chris grew even more frantic in both his movements and speech patterns.

He started wringing his hands as if each were trying to peel the flesh from the other from their sheer force of friction. Within the span of just a few minutes, he'd experienced three separate phenomena so extreme that any one of them would suggest either Chris was suffering from a sudden, dangerous medical condition or the presence of powerful supernatural or paranormal forces.

Dante grasped Chris' other shoulder and guided him in the direction of the living room. As they entered the larger, more open area, Dante spotted the closest couch to sit his brother down upon. He'd only just shifted their course towards it when first, there came the desperate plea of an older man in obvious, immediate danger:

"PLEEEASSE!! HELP ME!! THIS CRAZY MAN!! TRYING TO KILL MM-EE!! OPEN THE DOOR!!"

Followed by the man initiating a hailstorm of fists that sounded as if he had no intention of stopping until his cries were answered.

Lord Charon lay on his side, using the edge of the sidewalk to keep the left side of his body higher than the right. Most of the wounds he sustained in his battle with Arsenikos were there, so this was the best he could manage as far as elevating them. It hardly mattered. That first strike, the one sustained to his midsection, was a death blow in of itself.

Once he'd extracted the sharpened rod from his torso, his blood drained out like wine from a cracked jug. On this plane, with not a single other member of his kind present, he was as close to mortal as one could be. Hades had told him it would be so. It hadn't prepared him for how it would feel, however. He felt the world turn about his head and spine as if he were the axis upon which they spun, and knew that it was likely he would die here.

He regained himself in time to land five, maybe six blows upon Arsenikos, but once time had resumed, these only seemed to galvanize him. Arsenikos, the word for male and masculine, was no man at all. The male in of itself should not be allowed to exist, else he be poison to all those around him.

Lord Charon could not match the monster. Within seconds, he had been forced to capitulation, left to die in the street.

Would he see Thanatos again? The mere promise of hearing his voice, his humor again was enough. Maybe this was good, then. Maybe it was time.

But when tempered, combined in the correct proportions like his coins, became something greater than either. The bronze that appeared silver.

By the dull yellow lamp above him, and through the green of his welder's goggles, the liquid appeared dark purple as it pooled into a vaguely circular shape before him on the street. The color reminded him of the name the Romans had given him, after that most distant of planets, Pluto.

"Night's Plutonian Shore..." he whispered as his eyes began to flutter, to waver.

Lord Charon had always known that the word 'immortal' was merely for show, a stupid boast made by stupid gods and goddesses convinced of the lie and drunk on themselves.

Perhaps it was finally his time. There was relief, because were it to be true, there would no more of it for him.

Time.

The man at their door, older for sure but by no means senile or frail physically, looked exactly like an individual who had in fact just been violently attacked by a serial killer.

Wounds covered his entire body, looking as if he had been struck in an alarmingly large number of spots with some kind of one-handed pick/hammer/axe. Seven, eight, maybe even ten times. How he had managed to pull himself away from his attacker *and* maintain consciousness was nothing short of a miracle.

Or the wounds weren't nearly as severe as he let on.

"He had on green welder's goggles, and horns! There are horns coming from his head! Please, you have to get me away from him!"

Once Dante had opened the door, the man did not cease even for a moment relaying his horrific, disjointed, one-sentence accounts of his encounter with this maniac just moments before. Dante had attended to the man upon seeing him laying upon their doorstep, awash with bloodstains, filthy with partial blunt force and piercing wounds, each racing to see which one would achieve a full hemorrhagic state first.

Chris, for his part, didn't move a single muscle nor limb for a solid two to three minutes. Instead, he simply locked his eyes onto the man and never wavered in his vigilance.

This man, who supposedly had been attacked and seriously injured by a psychopath just moments earlier, managed still to have the strength to drag himself away, then beat on their front door for a solid minute, and at last launch into the shuffle mode of an "every pathetic plea" playlist.

At last, he got up from the couch and paced over to the front steps where Dante and the man were.

Chris leaned down, directly into his face.

"Which direction, sir?"

Arsenikos looked up into the second brother's eyes and saw something within that took him aback, but for less than an instant. Arsenikos vaguely nodded in no real direction at all.

Chris stood back away from the bleeding man, fully upright.

He turned from them and began to walk back out towards where he and Dante had parked.

"Jesus, dude! Didn't you hear the guy? Serial killer on the -"

"I'll be okay, Dante. Just want to see what's up out here."

Dante yelled out after him.

"Fucking be careful, alright? I..."

Chris had already walked too far and around to the front side of one of the condos to hear those last two words from his brother Dante.

Eventually, Chris came upon Charon laying in the street, yards from where he'd parked his vehicle, nearly every drop of his blood having drained out onto the pavement.

Some serial killer.

Instinctively, Chris reached down and touched the man's horns. The instant his fingers made contact, he experienced yet another vision – this time it was...

no! Dante! nooooooooooooooooooo....

Arsenikos had opened his brother Dante's throat using his father's coin, of all things.

And then, as seen through the eyes of Lord Charon:

Thanatos!!! nooooooooooooo........

Charon looked up at the boy and realized in that instant why it was he saw nothing in his soul earlier that evening. It explained both the familiarity and the alien aspect of Chris' soul.

Christ. Charon.

For the first time in all of his existence, Charon gazed upon his own avatar. And in Chris' presence, Charon was rejuvenated once more, for gods could and would always be immortal in the presence of their heroes of legend; their deeds performed in their patron diety's name.

He began to regain himself, to stand. Chris put his hand on his shoulder.

"Stay down. He's mine."

Chris grabbed one of the *sagaris* from a section of pavement near where Charon lay. He turned around, spotted a line of shrubs planted in the front yard of the condominium, and headed towards it.

"Chris, those are not meant to be thrown. I can –"

"They are now. Play dead, old man."

Moments later, Arsenikos returned. He hunkered down over Charon, fingering what had been Dante's coin, now stained with the dead brother's blood.

"I'll find the other one soon enough, *Lord Charon*. Your little time-stopping stunts aside, I -did- enjoy the challenge, however small."

Arsenikos considered the coin once more, turning it around in his hands.

"Does this mean that this coin is worthless now that you're dead, Charon?"

Arsenikos tossed the coin aside, its value and signifcance rendered meaningless in his estimation of the ferryman's current lifeless state.

"I must see the face of the god who tried and failed to stop me. They say to look upon it will bring instant madness to any who regard it."

Arsenikos pulled the goggles and mask off Charon's head. When he saw the face beneath, he sat silent for a moment...and then began to laugh. Hysterically.

"Oh my word. Look at you. Pathetic, like every filthy whore I ended all those years ago."

There was nothing about Charon's countenance that was remarkable or unusual save for one thing. Though his eyes were closed, tears ran from them as if they belonged to a person in the throes of crying or weeping. Arsenikos' laughter came at the idea that despite this fraud of a deity being nothing more than so much meat rotting in a road, it still cried as a weakling would: scared, frightened, afraid, and alone.

Arsenikos finally ceased his braying to address the figure beneath him a final time.

"I wonder. Should I fashion my new mask from *your* face, Lord Charon?"

At his asking, Charon's eyes popped open, with the light that burned within them brighter than they had been in centuries. Their violet hues were nearly blinding.

Arsenikos' heart dropped into his feet with the weight of equal parts of pure shock and abject fear.

"I wouldn't know, Arsenikos. Why don't you ask my avatar?"

Arsenikos' own eyes popped wide open, the whites actually visible. No longer were they twin spheres of oblivion.

He then heard a high-pitched, whirring sound, like metal spinning the air. Arsenikos had time to think:

One of his sagaris. But they couldn't be thrown with any -

And as if to refute the assertion before Arsenikos could finish it, the weapon's head buried itself within his spinal column from behind, paralyzing him instantly. He let out a sickening *UUURRK* sound when it landed and then fell over to the ground.

"Cunt," finished Charon.

It was over. Charon and Christos stood over
Arsenikos' body.

Charon asked:

"What will you do with your prize, my boy?"

Charon already regarded this mortal as an
adopted son. His prodigy-level skill with the *sagaris*
would have earned even Thanatos' respect. Chris
extended his left hand, as if to ask to borrow the
other for just a moment.

Chris' throw had hit its target dead center,
striking between the third and fourth vertebrae, and
had paralyzed Arsenikos from the neck down
instantaneously.

Arsenikos was still alive...but only barely.

Chris softly, surely drifted over to him...

And with one swing buried the second *sagaris* in
his skull, ending him instantly.

Lord Charon grunted. It was done. But then:

Christos then tore the first sagaris from his spine,
And then tore the second out from his skull,
And into his prone corpse, buried each into a kidney;
He lifted the one known as Arsenikos entirely from the ground;
So that no part of him touched the earth
and in raising him from the earth
raised him back to earth
but not as himself
but only
a hole
where a person should be.

Charon could not believe what he had just seen; if the *sagaris* could still wield power over the dead, it meant that Thanatos was not gone.

He was *somewhere*.

Before he could react to this knowledge, the boy had turned to him and asked:

"Wanna help me with this piece of shit, Lord Charon?"

Charon had thought it was his destiny to die upon this ground, but instead, he, the boy, and the piece of shit would all be reborn...

...here upon Night's Plutonian Shore.

Charon replied:

"I would be so honored."

Underneath eleven feet of earth, Arsenikos would spend the future, untold aeons of earth laying upon his back, with eyes open, until the earth would be swallowed by the sun. Nothing in that entire duration would ever change in his surroundings.

Arsenikos would forget Time.

Arsenikos would forget Death.

He would never be able to forget again, however, and become Andreas of Anywhere.

He would always remember that he was...

Nothing.

Lord Charon stood before him, his eyes once again covered by the welder's goggles, restored to vitality in the presence of an avatar – his first. Chris handed the *sagaris* back to Charon. Charon refused one of them, insisting Chris keep it.

"My brother... wherever he is... favors you. This belongs to you, now."

Chris' eyes were no longer ablaze not with fury, vengeance, or anger. He was no longer afraid of dying himself, for Chris would welcome joining both his father and brother in the next life. Charon gazed deep into the boy's eyes. The light that once burned in his own, the one the legends had said driven him mad incalculable eons ago -perhaps as early as his birth was something primordial. But madness? No.

Unending. Unceasing. It was then that Chris had learned what no mortal ever had in all of existence.

"My Lord Charon, you are not the god of death. "

"I am not the god of death – never have been. This has been the great sorrow of my existence, one that no mortal has ever been able to see the truth therein."

Chris wondered if he would also be the last.

"Maybe that was always for the best."

Chris steeled himself before he spoke his next words, knowing they could bring him doom the likes of which had never before been felt by any being who had walked upon the earth.

"You are the god of time."

Charon responded, as if in prayer, or mass.

"And you are its first hero. Remember what that means, Christos."

"I will serve. I will suffer."

"I can't give you your brother back, Christos. I wish that I could."

Lord Charon stuck his hand out. Chris took it.

"Goodbye Christos Poulos. I will look in on you, from time to time."

Chris could make out the features of a grin underneath his mask.

"Goodbye, my - " To his left, the snap of a broken branch cough his attention. Chris looked in its direction and saw nothing. He looked back...

...but Charon was gone.

"Screwed that up, Chris," he said to himself and began to leave the condo complex on foot, ahead of him, the rest of a life now uncertain and never to be perfected like he had done before.

He stopped at the condominium entrance. He considered who he was now – what he was now the champion of...and said out loud:

"I figured out what I'm left with now, Dante."

ΑΦΤΕΡΩΟΡΔ

My older brother and father passed away in 2016 and 2019, respectively. Each of them would have lived a bit longer, had they not spent a large part of their lives destroying themselves – and each other.

And I have been left to try to make sense of why they're gone, and why they hated each other so much.

Neither Michael nor my father could be considered even remotely malicious, evil, or aberrant people. Both were kind, funny, genuine people in of themselves. Were it Michael and myself spending time together, or my father and I, we were aces. I have found memories of each of my individual relationships with both that I choose to hang onto, rather than those times when they (my brother and father) would quite literally try to kill each other.

Were you to ask anyone 'in the know' with my family's troubles, each person's answer would undoubtedly kick off with their issues with addiction. It's easy for those without those struggles to point to them as the root cause of their troubles. And, without question, those problems did not help the situation; indeed exacerbating their conflicts into the...well, let's face it - bloodthirsty violence that erupted between them more times than I could ever possibly count.

But I have had and struggled with those very same issues, and yet I never fought with either on the scale of sheer ferocity and anger that they all too often would reach in their conflicts. So, whereas each of our struggles with substance abuse issues certainly didn't help matters, that is *not* where they came from.

Addiction, and alcoholism, as anyone in any recovery program will tell you, are the debilitating symptoms or manifestations of something much, much deeper that is wrong with an individual. The most compelling evidence for this fact is the work of Johann Hari, whose work – and experimental results – is so profoundly striking it is simply folly to ignore. I have found that his statement "the opposite of addiction is not sobriety, it is human connection" is more than opinion, but proven fact.

My brother lost his father at the age of six in a terrible building disaster. My father had a laundry list of issues coming in to our little unit; but I think that what he wanted more than anything was a family of his own and not the one he was *in loco parentis* with the one he grew up in.

That's where it started – and that, kind reader, is where I am going to leave it. They needed help. Neither one was capable of it on their own.

They never received any either.

And so it got worse. And they got worse as well.

But therein lies the problem:

Why couldn't they resolve their bullshit on their own? Why was it so impossible for them to just come to their senses, even just for twenty-four hours, and say to themselves 'alright, we can't keep putting holes in walls and having the police show up once a week' and just agree to fucking disagree?

And this question is what lay of the heart of "ἀρσενικός", which is a question that speaks to the fundamental broken-ness of being male, masculine, and fulfilling what is expected of us in society.

Gentlemen, we are fucking broken. In a whole lotta ways. Every single one of us, to one extent or another, is an internal combustion machine powered by those emotions and feelings we've been taught to keep inside, leave unexpressed or kept to ourselves, or ignore. The worst part of this happy dynamic is that even the 'enlightened' world of today, when those of us lucky enough to find ourselves in relationships that support that kind or level of self-expression, its only half-assed, in moderation type deals. "Yes, honey, that's good that you're opening up to me. But not right now, okay?"

I believe that we don't know what to do with ourselves anymore, because the rest of the world no longer knows what to do with us anymore.

And to this I say, fine. Call us when y'all figure it out. I've seen far, far too many instances now of men who do communicate, who do express themselves on genuine, honest terms and for their troubles are invariably walked over, discarded, or thrown out. They're the constantly leaned on, the ones who get the phone calls from hurt friends whenever they need a shoulder to cry upon, but whenever these guys need someone to talk to or genuine affection or love? Fucking crickets.

My brother's and father's lack of human connection wasn't just in relation to each other. They weren't getting it from other, essential, vital sources within our family.

And this dynamic, when it happens to be extreme enough in certain circumstances as to require the lens of abnormal psychology... regarding men with *severely* dysfunctional upbringings? This is when and where serial killers are typically born, friends and neighbors.

So, it should it come to no-one's surprise that maltreatment at the hands of our female (and others that fill that role) family members falls upon a spectrum, and that spectrum – unless its specifically violent - is one generally ignored once outside that extreme lens?

As for me?

Well, my life went sideways a long, long time ago and it's been damage control, more-or-less, ever since. It's only now, really, that I've stopped walking around with a guilty conscience because I didn't see or speak to Michael really for the eight years prior to his death in 2016. Of course, I wish that I had that time back, had seen the truth of things faster. But rather beat myself up for the rest of time because that had happened, instead I am grateful for the times we did have together.

We had some really good times together.

The same goes for my father. I wish that I could have or return the same level of love and affection he had for me, his only son – but watching him leave once or twice a year or four to eight months over and over again has an effect on a kid. I had to maintain a distance from him so that I wouldn't have to endure that same level of emotional pain each time.

Lastly –

See those two paragraphs up there?

I wish I could have expressed those sentiments to each of them. Michael needed to know that being in his company could be, and often was – a great thing.

My father needed to know why his son seemed so distant sometimes, and that it wasn't his fault. At all.

But somewhere, in one part of the Elysian Fields, they know. And there, I hope, they wait for me. But until that day, well...

...I will in some part, in my own way, act as Charon's avatar not because I am alone, disconnected, broken, or otherwise not what others expect me to be.

It is what I choose to be.

At least until the world can make up its mind on what to do with me. Or us.

I'm not holding my fucking breath, gentlemen.

-w.p. Quigley, *March 2024*

ΣΠΕΧΙΑΛ ΤΗΑΝΚΣ / ΑΧΚΝΟΩΛΕΔΓΕΜΕΝΤΣ

Of all the myriad flavors, genres, and influences on this weird little work, none were more influential or comprised more of its integral DNA than the cheeseburger, fries, and coke of the horror world:

the slasher film.

For this, I want to thank and acknowledge those directors that pioneered and elevated the idea of just having a maniac run-down victims in no particular order onscreen for an hour and a half and somehow making it art:

Alfred Hitchcock, "Psycho"
Mario Bava, "Bay of Blood"
John Carpenter, "Halloween"
Wes Craven, "A Nightmare on Elm Street"
Sean S. Cunningham, "Friday the 13th"

Paul Cockburn, for his time, wisdon, and energy in editing and providing his advice and knowledge to help this work become reality.

And without too much more gladhandling, I also want to thank my brothers whom I have chosen and who have chosen me as such. We look after each other, and must – for surely no one else will the way that only brothers can.

9 781963 970029